WHERE
THE
MOUNTAIN
MEETS
THE MOON

This wonderful book was provided to our HWRSD families free of charge because of a generous grant from Luso Federal Credit Union and the Joseph Dias Jr. Estate Al Trust Foundation. Thank you.

WHERE THE MOUNTAIN MEETS THE MOON

Grace Lin

LITTLE, BROWN AND COMPANY
NEW YORK BOSTON

Little, Brown and Company

Hachette Book Group
1290 Avenue of the Americas, New York, NY 10104
Visit our website at www.lb-kids.com

Little, Brown and Company is a division of Hachette Book Group, Inc.
The Little, Brown name and logo are trademarks of Hachette Book Group, Inc.

The publisher is not responsible for websites (or their content) that are not owned by the publisher.

First Paperback Edition: April 2011
First published in hardcover in June 2009 by Little, Brown and Company

Where the Mountain Meets the Moon Educator's Guide prepared by Jennifer McMahon

Lin, Grace.
  Where the mountain meets the moon / by Grace Lin.—1st ed.
    p. cm.
  Summary: Minli, an adventurous girl from a poor village, buys a magical goldfish, and then joins a dragon who cannot fly on a quest to find the Old Man of the Moon in hopes of bringing life to Fruitless Mountain and freshness to Jade River.
  ISBN 978-0-316-11427-1 (hc) / ISBN 978-0-316-03863-8 (pb)
  [1. Fairy tales.   2. Dragons—Fiction.   3. Moon—Fiction.]   I. Title.
  PZ8.L6215Whe 2009
  [Fic]—dc22

                                                                                    2008032818

20 19 18 17 16 15 14 13 12

RRD-C

Book design by Alison Impey

Printed in the United States of America

FOR ROBERT

SPECIAL THANKS TO:

ALVINA, CONNIE, LIBBY, JANET, MOM, DAD, AND ALEX

CHAPTER

1

Far away from here, following the Jade River, there was once a black mountain that cut into the sky like a jagged piece of rough metal. The villagers called it Fruitless Mountain because nothing grew on it and birds and animals did not rest there.

Crowded in the corner of where Fruitless Mountain and the Jade River met was a village that was a shade of faded brown. This was because the land around the village was hard and poor. To coax rice out of the stubborn land, the fields had to be flooded with water. The villagers had to tramp in the mud, bending and stooping and planting day after day. Working in the mud so much made it spread everywhere and the hot sun dried it onto their clothes and hair and homes. Over time, everything in the village had become the dull color of dried mud.

One of the houses in this village was so small that its wood boards, held together by the roof, made one think of a bunch of matches tied with a piece of twine. Inside, there was barely enough room for three people to sit around the table — which was lucky because only three people lived there. One of them was a young girl called Minli.

Minli was not brown and dull like the rest of the village. She had glossy black hair with pink cheeks, shining eyes always eager for adventure, and a fast smile that flashed from her face. When people saw her lively and impulsive spirit, they thought her name, which meant *quick thinking,* suited her well. "Too well," her mother sighed, as Minli had a habit of quick acting as well.

Ma sighed a great deal, an impatient noise usually accompanied with a frown at their rough clothes, rundown house, or meager food. Minli could not remember a time when Ma did not sigh; it often made Minli wish she had been called a name that meant *gold* or *fortune* instead. Because Minli and her parents, like the village and the land around them, were very poor. They were barely able to harvest enough rice to feed themselves, and the only money in the house was two old copper coins that sat in a blue rice bowl with a white rabbit painted on it. The coins and the bowl belonged to Minli; they had been given to her when she was a baby, and she had had them for as long as she could remember.

What kept Minli from becoming dull and brown like the rest of the village were the stories her father told her every night at dinner. She glowed with such wonder and excitement that even Ma would smile, though she would shake her head at the same time. Ba seemed to drop his gray and work weariness — his black eyes sparkled like raindrops in the sun when he began a story.

"Ba, tell me the story about Fruitless Mountain again," Minli would say as her mother spooned their plain rice into bowls. "Tell me again why nothing grows on it."

"Ah," Minli's father said, "you've heard this so many times. You know."

"Tell me again, Ba," Minli begged. "Please."

"Okay," he said, and as he set down his chopsticks his smile twinkled in a way that Minli loved.

 # THE STORY OF FRUITLESS MOUNTAIN

O nce when there were no rivers on the earth, the Jade Dragon was in charge of clouds. She decided when and where the clouds would rain upon the land and when they would stop. She was very proud of her power and of the reverence the people of earth paid her. Jade Dragon had four dragon children: Pearl, Yellow, Long, and Black. They were large and strong and good and kind. They helped Jade Dragon with her work, and whenever they flew in the sky she was overwhelmed with love and pride.

However, one day, as Jade Dragon ended the rain and moved the clouds away from the land, she overheard some villagers' conversation.

"Ah, thank goodness the rain is gone," one man said.

"Yes," another said, "I'm so tired of the rain. I'm glad the clouds are gone and the sun is finally shining."

Those words filled Jade Dragon with anger. Tired of rain! Glad the clouds were gone! Jade Dragon was indignant. How dare the villagers dishonor her that way!

Jade Dragon was so offended that she decided that she would never let it rain again. "The people can enjoy the sun forever," Jade Dragon thought resentfully.

Of course, that meant despair for the people on earth. As the sun beat overhead and the rain never came, drought and famine spread over the land. Animals and trees withered and died and the people begged for rain, but Jade Dragon ignored them.

But their suffering did not go unnoticed by Jade Dragon's children. They were horrified at the anguish and misery on earth. One by one, they went to their mother and pleaded forgiveness for the humans — but even their words did not soften their mother's cold heart. "We will never make it rain for the people again," Jade Dragon vowed.

Pearl, Yellow, Long, and Black met in secret.

"We must do something to help the people," Black said. "If they do not get water soon, they will all die."

"Yes," Yellow said, "but what can we do? We cannot make it rain. We cannot dishonor Mother with disobedience."

Long looked down at the earth. "I will sacrifice myself for the people of earth," he said. "I will lie on the land and transform myself into water for them to drink."

The others looked at him in astonishment, but one by one they nodded.

"I will do the same," Yellow said.

"As will we," Pearl and Black said.

So Jade Dragon's children went down to earth and turned themselves into water, saving the people on the earth. They became the four great rivers of the land, stopping the drought and death of all those on earth.

But when Jade Dragon saw what her children had done, she cursed herself for her pride. No longer would her dragon children fly in the air with her or call her Mother. Her heart broke in grief and sadness; she fell from the sky and turned herself into the Jade River in hopes that she could somehow be reunited with her children.

Fruitless Mountain is the broken heart of Jade Dragon. Nothing grows or lives on the mountain; the land around it is hard and the water of the river is dark because Jade Dragon's sad spirit is still there. Until Jade Dragon is no longer lonely and is reunited with at least one of her children, Fruitless Mountain will remain bare.

"Why doesn't someone bring the water of the four great rivers to the mountain?" Minli asked, even though she had asked this question many times before. Every time Ba told the story, she couldn't help thinking how wonderful it would be to have the mountain blooming with fruit and flowers, bringing richness to their needy village. "Wouldn't that make Jade Dragon happy?"

"When Jade Dragon's children turned themselves into water," Minli's father said, "they were at peace and their spirits were released. Their spirits are no longer in the water. So Jade Dragon cannot find them in the rivers.

Over a hundred years ago, a man tried to reunite them by taking stones from the mountain to the rivers."

"That man was not taking the stone for a dragon spirit," Minli's mother cut in. She never quite approved of Ba's stories, as she felt they made Minli impractical and caused her to daydream. "My grandmother told me he was an artist. He took the mountain rock to carve into inking stones."

"Did he ever come back?" Minli asked.

"No. It probably did not make good ink." Ma sighed. "He probably found something finer elsewhere. I bet the bronze on his horse's saddle was more than we will ever have."

Ma's sighs made Minli wish that every rock of Fruitless Mountain were gold and she couldn't help asking, "So how will Fruitless Mountain ever grow green again?"

"Ah," her father said, "that is a question you will have to ask the Old Man of the Moon."

"Oh, tell that story next!" Minli begged. "Whenever I ask something important, people say, 'That is a question you have to ask the Old Man of the Moon.' Someday, I will ask him."

"The Old Man of the Moon! Another story! Our house

is bare and our rice hardly fills our bowls, but we have plenty of stories." Ma sighed again. "What a poor fortune we have!"

"Maybe," Ba said to Minli, glancing at Ma, "I should tell you that story tomorrow."

CHAPTER

2

Every morning, before the sun rose, Minli, her mother, and her father began work in the fields. It was planting season, which was especially grueling. The mud stuck to their feet like glue and each seedling had to be painstakingly planted by hand. When the hot sun burned overhead, Minli's knees shook from weariness. She hated the feeling of thick, soggy mud on her hands and face; and many times she wanted to stop in irritation and exhaustion. But seeing her parents patiently working, backs bent, made her swallow her complaints and continue.

As soon as the sun began to set, Minli's parents sent her home to make dinner and to rest while they continued to work in the thick mud. They would not come home until the sun had completely disappeared from the sky.

At home, Minli washed her face and hands and feet; and even though all the water in the basin turned brown, she still felt like she was covered in mud. Her arms and legs were so tired that she felt like an old crab crawling on rocks. As she looked at herself reflected in the dark water, she saw Ma's frown on her face.

Ma is right, Minli thought. *What a poor fortune we have. Every day, Ba and Ma work and work and we still have nothing. I wish I could change our fortune.*

At that very moment, Minli heard a faint murmuring sound that she had never heard before, like a song chanted from the clouds. Curious, she opened the door to see what the noise was.

And there, on the road in front of her house, she saw a small stranger calling out quietly. "Goldfish," he was saying softly, as if he were coaxing his fish to swim. "Bring fortune into your home."

Minli and the villagers stared as he wheeled his cart.

Even though the village was by a river, it had been many years since anyone had seen a glimpse of a goldfish. The fish in the Jade River were brown and gray, like the village. The goldfish man's cart was full of bowls of flashing fish that glittered like jewels.

His gentle calling drew Minli to him like a moth to a lit lantern. "How does a goldfish bring fortune into your home?" Minli asked.

The goldfish man looked at her; the sun setting behind him made him glow bright red and yellow. "Don't you know?" he asked her. "Goldfish means plenty of gold. Having a bowl of goldfish means your house will be full of gold and jade."

As Minli stared into his bowls with her shining black eyes, a brilliant orange fish stared back at her with its shining black eyes. And then quickly, so quickly that Minli barely thought about it, she turned into the house and grabbed the two copper coins from the white rabbit rice bowl.

"I'll buy that one," Minli said, and she pointed at the fiery orange fish with the black eyes and fin that had caught her eye.

The other village children looked at her enviously while the watching adults shook their heads. "Minli," one neighbor said, "don't believe his impossible talk. A goldfish won't bring fortune. Save your money."

But Minli was not discouraged and she held out her copper coins to the goldfish man. He looked at her and smiled. Then he took one coin, picked up the fishbowl, and gave it to her.

"May it bring you great fortune," he said. And with a small bow to the villagers, he wheeled out of the village. In moments, he disappeared from view into the shadow of Fruitless Mountain, and if it wasn't for the goldfish Minli had in her hands, all would have thought he was a dream.

CHAPTER

3

But the goldfish was real, and when her parents returned from the fields for dinner they were not happy to learn that Minli had spent her money on it.

"How could you spend your money on that!" Ma said, slapping the rice bowls on the table. "On something so useless? And we will have to feed it! There is barely enough rice for us as it is."

"I will share my rice with it," Minli said quickly. "The goldfish man said that it will bring fortune to our house."

"Fortune!" Ma said. "You spent half the money in our house!"

"Now, Wife," Ba said, sitting quietly, "it was Minli's money. It was hers to do with as she wished. Money must be used sometime. What use is money in a bowl?"

"It is more useful than a goldfish in a bowl," her mother said shortly.

"Who knows," Ba said. "Maybe it will bring fortune to our house."

"Another impossible dream," Ma said, looking at the plain rice in her bowl with bitterness. "It will take more than a goldfish to bring fortune to our house."

"Like what?" Minli asked. "What do we need to bring fortune here?"

"Ah," Ba said, "that is a question you will have to ask the Old Man of the Moon."

"The Old Man of the Moon again," Minli said, and she looked at her father. "Ba, you said you would tell me the Old Man of the Moon story again today."

"More stories!" Ma said, and her chopsticks struck the inside of her empty rice bowl resentfully. "Haven't we had enough of those?"

"Now, Wife," Ba said again, "stories cost us nothing."

"And gain us nothing as well," Ma said.

There was a stony silence as Ba looked sadly into his rice bowl. Minli tugged at his sleeve. "Please, Ba?" she said.

Ma shook her head and sighed, but said nothing, so Ba began.

THE STORY OF THE OLD MAN OF THE MOON

Once there was a magistrate who was quite powerful and proud. He was so proud that he demanded constant respect from his people. Whenever he made a trip out of the city, no matter what time of day or night, people were to leave their homes, get on their knees, and make deep bows as he passed, or else face the brutal punishment of his soldiers. The magistrate was fierce in his anger as well as his pride. It is said he even expected the monkeys to come down from the trees to bow to him.

The magistrate was harsh with his subordinates, ruthless to his enemies, and pitiless to his people. All feared his wrath, and when he roared his orders the people trembled. Behind his back, they called him Magistrate Tiger.

Magistrate Tiger's most coveted wish was to be of royal blood. His every decision was crafted for that purpose; every manipulation was part of a strategy to achieve acceptance into the imperial family. As soon as his son was born, he began to make trips and inquiries to gain influence, in hopes that he could marry his son to a member of the imperial family.

One night, as the magistrate traveled through the mountains (again on a trip to gain favor for his son's future marriage), he saw an old man sitting alone in the moonlight. The old man ignored the passing horses and carriages, the silk brocade and the government seal, and simply continued reading a large book in his lap, placidly fingering a bag of red string beside him. The old man's indifference infuriated Magistrate Tiger and he ordered the carriage to stop. However, even the halting noises did not make the old man look up.

Finally, Magistrate Tiger exited his carriage and went to the old man, who was still engrossed in his book.

"Do you not bow to your magistrate?!" he roared.

The old man continued to read.

"What are you reading that is so important?" the magistrate demanded, and looked at the pages of the book. It was full of scribbles and scrawls that were not of any language the magistrate knew of. "Why, it's just nonsense written in there!"

"Nonsense!" the old man said, finally looking up. "You fool. This is the Book of Fortune. It holds all the knowledge of the world — the past, present, and future."

The magistrate looked again at the marks on the page. "I cannot read it," he said.

"Of course not," the man said. "But I, the Old Man of the Moon, Guardian of the Book of Fortune, can read it. And with it, I can answer any question in the world."

"You can answer any question in the world?" the magistrate scoffed. "Very well. Who will my son marry when he is of age?"

The Old Man of the Moon flipped the pages of the book. "Hmm," he said to himself. "Yes, here it is . . . your son's future wife is now the two-year-old daughter of a grocer in the next village."

"The daughter of a grocer!" the magistrate spat.

"Yes," the Old Man of the Moon continued. "Right now she is wrapped in a blue blanket embroidered with white rabbits, sitting on the lap of her blind grandmother in front of her house."

"No!" the magistrate said. "I won't allow it!"

"It's true," the Old Man said. "They are destined to be husband and wife. I, myself, tied the red cord that binds them."

"What red cord?" Magistrate Tiger demanded.

"Do you know nothing? I tie together everyone who meets with these red threads." The Old Man sighed, holding up his bag full of red string. "When you were born, I tied your ankle to your wife's ankle with a red thread, and as you both grew older the line became shorter until you eventually met. All the people you've met in your life have been brought to you by the red cords I tied. I must have forgotten to tie the end of one of the lines, which is why you are meeting me now. I won't do that again."

"I don't believe you," the magistrate said.

"Believe or don't believe," the Old Man said, standing up and putting the big book on his back. "We have reached the end of our thread and I will now leave."

The magistrate stared in dumbfounded silence as the Old Man of the Moon walked away up the mountain.

"Crazy old man," the magistrate said finally. "What a waste of my time!"

The magistrate returned to his carriage and continued on. But as they drove through the next village, he saw an old blind woman holding a baby girl in front of a house. The girl was wrapped in a blue blanket embroidered with white rabbits, just as the Old Man of the Moon had said.

Magistrate Tiger burned with anger. "I will not let my son marry a grocer's daughter!" he vowed. So, after he arrived at his guesthouse, the magistrate secretly ordered one of his servants to return to the grocer's home and stab the girl with a knife. *That will take care of her,* he thought to himself.

Many years later, Magistrate Tiger had his dream fulfilled. He was finally able to obtain a match for his son with one of the emperor's many granddaughters, and his son would inherit the rule of a remote city. On the wedding day, Magistrate Tiger bragged to his son about how he had arranged the marriage and outwitted the Old Man of the Moon. The son (who was not like his father) said nothing, but after the wedding ceremony, sent a trusted servant to find the grocer's family to make amends. In the meantime, he became acquainted with his bride and was happy to find that both were pleased with each other. He found his new wife beautiful, the only oddity about her being that she always wore a delicate flower on her forehead.

"Dear Wife," he said, "why do you always wear that flower? Even to sleep, you never remove it."

"It is to hide my scar," she said, touching her forehead in embarrassment. "When I was a child no older than two, a strange man stabbed me with a knife. I survived, but I still have this scar."

And at that moment, the trusted servant came rushing in. "Master," he said, "I made the inquiries you asked for. In a flood many years ago, the grocer's family perished — except for the daughter. The king of the city (the emperor's ninth son) then adopted the daughter and raised her as his own . . . and that daughter is your wife!"

"So the Old Man of the Moon was right!" Minli said.

"Of course he was," Ba replied. "The Old Man of the Moon knows everything and can answer any question you ask."

"I should ask him how to bring fortune to our house!" Minli said. "He would know, I'll ask him. Where do I find him?"

"They say he lives on top of Never-Ending Mountain," Ba said. "But no one I have ever spoken to knows where that is."

"Maybe we can find out," Minli said.

"Oh, Minli!" Ma said impatiently. "Bringing fortune to our house! Making Fruitless Mountain bloom! You're always wishing to do impossible things! Stop believing stories and stop wasting your time."

"Stories are not a waste of time," Ba said.

"Stories," Ma said, slapping her hands against the table, making the water in the fishbowl sway as she stood up and left the table, "are what wasted money on this goldfish."

Minli stared down at her rice bowl; the few white grains left sat like precious pearls at the bottom of her bowl. Ba patted her arm. "Eat all your rice, Daughter," he said, and with his shaking hands, he scooped the last of his own rice to feed the fish.

CHAPTER
4

That night Minli could not sleep. Ma's words echoed in her ears and when she closed her eyes she saw Ba's hand, shaking from hard work, feeding the goldfish.

Ma is right, Minli thought to herself. *The goldfish is just another mouth to feed. I can't let Ba feed the goldfish. Ma and Ba work so hard for every grain of rice, Ba shouldn't have to feed the goldfish too.*

Minli slipped quietly out of her bed and crept to the table where the goldfish was. They stared at each other and Minli knew what she had to do. Quickly slipping on her shoes and jacket, she took the goldfish and left the house.

It was late. The village was quietly asleep and the stars above filled the sky like spilled salt on dried seaweed. Minli's footsteps seemed to hush the night as she made her way toward the Jade River.

At the edge of the river, Minli looked at her goldfish one last time. The moon shone above so even in the darkness of the night, the fish seemed to burn a bright orange. Its black eyes sparkled at her.

"I'm sorry I can't keep you," Minli whispered. "I hope you will be all right in the river." And with those words, she emptied the bowl into the water. For a moment the fish seemed shocked and was still, like a flickering flame on a match. Then it wiggled in the water and swam in circles, a joyful fire twirling in the water.

Minli watched it and sighed. As the sound faded into the night, Minli realized it was an echo of her mother's impatient, frustrated noise. "Ma will never stop sighing unless our fortune changes. But how will it ever change?" Minli asked ruefully. "I guess that is just another question for the Old Man of the Moon. Too bad no one knows how to get to Never-Ending Mountain to ask him anything."

The fish stopped swimming and looked up at Minli.

"I know where it is," it said. The female voice was high and soft, like the wind whistling through the reeds of the water.

Minli stared. "Did you say something?" she asked.

"Yes," the fish said. "I know how you can get to Never-Ending Mountain and ask the Old Man of the Moon a question."

"You're a talking fish?" Minli asked, her words tumbling into each other with excitement. "How can you talk?"

"Most fish talk," the fish said, "if you are willing to listen. One, of course, must want to hear."

"I do," Minli said, enthralled and eager. This was just like one of Ba's stories! She bubbled with excitement. "How do you know the way to Never-Ending Mountain?"

"I've swum all the oceans and rivers, except for one," the fish said, "and on my way to the last, the goldfish man caught me. I despaired in his cart, for I have seen and learned much of the world, including the way to

Never-Ending Mountain. Since you have set me free, I will tell you."

"You've swum all the oceans and rivers?" Minli asked. The questions spilled like overflowing water. "Which river haven't you seen? Why have you traveled so much? Where is Never-Ending Mountain? When did —"

"This river is the one river I have not swum," the fish interrupted, "and I have waited a long time to see it. So I would like to start as soon as possible. You can ask the Old Man of the Moon all your other questions. Let me tell you the way to him so I can be off."

Minli nodded and asked no more. She realized she was having a conversation with a goldfish, which was very unusual, so she decided to listen.

CHAPTER
5

The next morning, Minli felt as if her head was spinning with thoughts and plans. She was so busy thinking and plotting that she barely noticed her parents nodding sadly at each other when they saw the empty fishbowl. And in the fields, when Minli worked as if in a daze, her parents said nothing about her slow and messy planting.

When the sun began to set and Minli went home to make dinner, she quickly washed and made the rice. Then she set the table for two people, sat down, and wrote this note:

Dear Ma and Ba,

I am going to Never-Ending Mountain to ask the Old Man of the Moon how I can change our fortune. I might be away for many days, but don't worry. I will be fine. When I come back, we will be able to fill our house with gold and jade.

Love, your obedient daughter,
Minli

The obedient part isn't completely true, Minli thought to herself, as she knew her parents would not be happy to find her gone. *But it's not false either. They didn't say I couldn't go, so I'm not being disobedient.*

Still, Minli knew that wasn't entirely right either. But she shook away her uneasy feelings and prepared for her journey. On a blanket, she put:

a needle

a pair of chopsticks

her white rabbit rice bowl

a small piece of dried bamboo

a hollow gourd full of water

a small knife

a fishnet

some uncooked rice

a large pot

and the one remaining copper coin

Then she wrapped her blanket into a bag, tied it on her back, and took a last look at the shabby house. Through the window, Fruitless Mountain stood like a shadow, but Minli closed her eyes and imagined the house shimmering with gold and the mountain jade green with trees, and smiled. Then, she opened the door and left.

CHAPTER

6

As Minli left the house, she was afraid some of her neighbors would stop her or ask where she was going. She felt she must look mysterious, with a large bag on her back and full of excitement. But no one noticed her. The neighbors kept sweeping their doorways, hanging their laundry, and preparing dinner. A boy and girl continued their fight over a pretend feast of mud. When the mother called them for dinner, both refused to move, each clinging to their dishes of wet dirt; Minli had to smile at their foolishness.

So Minli walked right out of the village without causing a second glance. At the edge of the village, she turned toward Fruitless Mountain.

At the bottom of the mountain, she unwrapped her blanket and took out her knife, needle, rice bowl, bamboo piece, and jug of water. Then, trying to remember all of the goldfish's instructions, she cracked off a small bit of stone and rubbed it up and down the needle ninety-nine times before tossing it back to the ground. Then she filled her rice bowl halfway with water and let the bamboo float in it. After that, she picked up the needle and looked at the white rabbit on her bowl.

"Okay," she said to the jumping rabbit, "lead the way." And she placed the needle onto the bamboo. Like magic, the needle spun around. Minli smiled.

"Thank you," Minli said again to the painted rabbit. "Now, I'll follow where you want me to go!"

Minli packed up her things and, carefully holding the bowl in her hand, walked in the direction of the needle, past Fruitless Mountain. "Goodbye, Jade Dragon," Minli said as she left. "When I come back I will know how to make you happy again!"

Minli walked and walked and the stony land slowly turned into forest. Even when the moon was high in the sky, she continued. "I want to make sure I walk far enough that if Ma and Ba begin to look for me, they can't find me," Minli said to herself. The fallen leaves made a soft carpet for her feet and the night birds flew into the sky as she passed. Only when the sky lightened to gray and the sun began to peek over the horizon did Minli sit down and rest against a tall tree. She had traveled deep into the forest, far from her village and her home. She was so tired that she quickly fell asleep.

CHAPTER
7

The sun had set and the moon was just beginning to rise in the sky when Ma and Ba returned home from the fields. Even though they could smell the steam from the rice cooking, they noticed the house was strangely dark and quiet.

"Why is Minli sitting in the darkness?" Ma wondered as they approached the house.

"Perhaps she is sad about giving up her goldfish," Ba said as he shook his head.

"Can our fortune be any poorer?" Ma sighed. "We cannot even feed a goldfish for our daughter."

But as Minli's parents entered the house and read her note, Ma made a noise like a shrieking cat.

"I spoke too soon," Ma cried. "Our fortune is now the worst, for our only daughter is gone!"

"Quiet, quiet, Wife," Ba hushed her. "If we move quickly, we can find her and bring her back home."

Ba hurriedly took out his cloth sack and gathered blankets and filled an empty bottle with water. "She has had almost half a day to travel ahead," he said. "It might take us some time to find her." Ma watched him and then began to pack the cooked rice into a traveling box. But she continued to weep. "It is all the stories you told her," Ma sobbed. "She believed them and now is looking for fairy tales."

Her words cut into Ba like slices from a knife but, even though his face was pained, he said nothing and continued to pack. His hands trembled as he tied the bag closed, but they were gentle when he put them on Ma's shoulders. "Let us go," he said.

As they left the house, many of their neighbors poked

their heads out their doors. They had heard Ma's scream through the thin walls of their closely spaced houses and wanted to know what had happened. When Ma and Ba told them, it seemed as if the whole village poured out from their homes.

"Never-Ending Mountain? The Old Man of the Moon? Changing your fortune?" the neighbors said. "You better go find her or else she will never return. Foolish Minli! She is trying to do the impossible!"

Each villager pointed and nodded toward the direction they had seen Minli last. Some had seen her heading home, others toward the rice fields. But finally, a small boy was heard. "Minli left toward Fruitless Mountain," he said. "I saw her with her pack. She went that way."

So with the villagers waving them goodbye, Ma and Ba walked toward Fruitless Mountain, their dark shadows trailing behind them in the moonlight. But when they reached the mountain, they looked at each other uncertainly.

"Where did she go from here?" Ba wondered, and he lit the lantern in his hand. The soft light seemed to warm the air and soften the growing darkness.

"Here!" Ma cried out, pointing to the ground. "There are footprints going toward the woods. Maybe they are Minli's!"

Ba looked at the footprints. There was another mark accompanying them, a long pulling line. Ba pointed at them, "But what is that?" he wondered.

"Maybe Minli was dragging a walking stick," Ma said. "The footprints could be hers."

Ba looked again at the footprints. They seemed small and nimble. "Perhaps they are," Ba said. "Let's follow them."

And so they did.

CHAPTER
8

Minli woke up when the sun was high in the sky and burning with light. Even in the shade of the forest, Minli's black head burned hot. As she woke up, she looked at her jug of water. Since she had used some of it for her compass and had drunk some during her night walk, it was only half full. She sipped it and tried not to think about Ma and Ba finding her note. "I hope they understand," Minli said to herself, shifting the weight of the water jug on her shoulders uncomfortably.

Minli walked west again. A couple of moments later,

she sipped her jug again. She tried to drink sparingly, but even through the leaves of the trees, the yellow sun glared down at her. Soon, her empty jug was bouncing against her arm when she heard a faint noise running through the trees.

"That's water trickling!" she said to herself as she turned toward the sound. "There's water here somewhere." Soon she noticed a small stream, running with clear, sparkling water. She eagerly bent down to drink and fill her jug, but as soon as Minli tasted the water she spit it out!

"Salt water!" Minli exclaimed. "This water is salty!"

As she sat back, Minli began to wonder, "How is this stream salty? I am far from the ocean. This is very strange." And unable to contain her curiosity, Minli forgot about her thirst and began to follow it.

The stream widened and deepened, becoming more of a river than a stream. Just as Minli began to think that she should return to her journey, she began to hear deep moans that gently shook the earth.

"Who's there?" Minli shouted.

"Help!" a muffled voice whimpered. "Can you help me?"

"I'm coming!" Minli called. She quickly put down her

compass on the side of the water and waded in. The water was warm, like bathwater, and clear as glass. Minli could see her feet and all the stones and leaves at the bottom of the stream. As she moved toward the voice, the water rose higher and higher, to her knees and then almost to her neck.

"Are you still there?" the voice asked plaintively. "Please help me!"

"I'm coming!" Minli called again. She took a deep breath and dove toward the voice. The salt water stung her eyes so she closed them tightly until she broke through the surface. When she finally opened her eyes, Minli almost sank back underwater with shock. Because there in front of her was . . . a DRAGON!

CHAPTER
9

Underneath the moon shadows of the trees, Ma stumbled with weariness. Ba did not know how long they had been walking. With every step he peered at the ground, the light flickering as the lantern swayed in his hand. The forest was full of shapes and shadows and only barely could he see the faint footprints on the ground — it was like searching for a wrinkle in a flower petal. As Ma tripped, he steadied her with his arm.

"We should rest," Ba said.

Ma shook her head and pulled away angrily. "We must keep going. We have to find Minli."

"But you are tired," Ba said, "and I am too. We can rest and afterward we will be able to continue faster."

"I am not tired," Ma said fiercely. Her irritation seemed to give her energy. "If you are tired, you can rest. But I will continue to look for our daughter."

"We should stay together," Ba said quietly.

"If you wish to stay with me," Ma said, "then you will have to keep going."

Ba sighed and took out another candle for the lantern. The light from the lamp kept away the forest animals but it could do nothing for Ma's fury. Her resentment seemed to darken with the fading moon.

But as they walked, the morning bloomed in the distance, its light slowly filtered over Ma and Ba through the veil of tree branches so he could finally blow out the candle in his lantern. He looked at Ma and could see that her bitterness was only sharper in the softening sky.

"If Minli stopped to rest," Ba said, "we may catch up with her soon."

"When we find her," Ma said, "she must know that she is never to do this again. Never!"

"Now, Wife," Ba said, "Minli did not leave to cause us harm."

"No," Ma said, her words cracking the air around her, "she left to find a fairy tale. Never-Ending Mountain and the Old Man of the Moon! Of all the foolish things."

"Stories are not foolish," Ba said again, in his quiet way.

"Says you!" Ma said. "Because you are the one who filled her with them. Making her believe she could change our miserable fortune with an impossible story! Ridiculous!"

"Yes," Ba said sadly, "it is impossible. But it is not ridiculous."

Ma opened her mouth again, but stopped. For up ahead there was a noise of breaking branches. It was the sound of someone pushing through the forest. Ma and Ba looked at each other. "Minli!" Ma said.

Forgetting their fatigue and frustration, Ma and Ba began to run through the woods. Ma ignored the branches that scratched her and Ba let his hat fall to the ground as they rushed toward the unseen person. "Minli!" they called, "Minli!"

But as they burst upon the figure ahead, they stopped in shock. It was not Minli. Instead, Ma and Ba stared openmouthed at the goldfish man.

CHAPTER

10

Minli gaped at the dragon in front of her. He was brilliant red, the color of a lucky lantern, with emerald-green whiskers, horns, and a dull stone-colored ball like the moon on his head. At least what Minli could see of him looked like that. Because he was also half-covered by ropes of twine that had been tied tightly around him so he couldn't move and by the silvery lake of water his tears had formed all around him.

Minli had always thought it would be thrilling but scary to meet a dragon. Her father's stories always made them sound so wise and powerful and grand. But here was a dragon before her, tied up and crying! Minli didn't feel awed by it at all. In fact, she felt rather sorry for it.

"Can you help me?" the dragon sniffled. "I am trapped."

Minli shook herself and started swimming toward the dragon. "What happened to you?" she asked.

"The monkeys tied me up while I was sleeping," the dragon said. "I have been here for days."

Minli swam over to the dragon and climbed onto his back to get out of the water. There, she opened her pack, took out the small, sharp knife she had brought with her, and started cutting the twine.

"Why did the monkeys tie you up?" Minli asked.

"Because I want to go farther into the forest to the peach grove," the dragon said, "and the monkeys will not let anyone through. I have been trying to make them let me pass peacefully for days, but they are so unreasonable. Finally I told them if they did not let me through, I would just force my way. They know I am big and strong enough to go through without their permission, so when I went to sleep, they tied me up."

"Why won't the monkeys let anyone pass?" Minli asked.

"Because they are greedy things," the dragon said. "They have just discovered the peach trees that make up the next part of the forest. The monkeys do not want to let anyone through because they do not want to share the peaches. Even when I promised not to touch any of the fruit, they would not let me through. They do not even want to share the sight of those peaches."

"Why do you have to go through the forest?" Minli asked. "Can't you just fly over?"

More tears, the size of lychee nuts, rolled down the dragon's face.

"I cannot fly," he sobbed. "I do not know why. All other dragons can fly. But I cannot. I wish I knew why."

"Don't cry," Minli said, patting the dragon, feeling more sorry for it than ever. "I'm going to Never-Ending Mountain to see the Old Man of the Moon and ask him how to change my family's fortune. You can come too and ask him how to fly."

"You know where Never-Ending Mountain is?" the

dragon asked. "I thought to see the Old Man of the Moon was impossible. You must be very wise to know how to find him."

"Not really," Minli said. "I got the directions from a goldfish."

CHAPTER
11

It took a long time for Minli to cut all the twine that bound the dragon. For some knots she had to swim underwater and cut through the waving grasses. As she popped in and out of the water, cutting, she told the dragon all about her village, the goldfish, and how she had just started her journey.

"I'm Minli," she said to the dragon. "What's your name?"

"Name?" the dragon asked slowly. "I do not think I have a name."

"Everyone has a name," Minli said. "When you were born, didn't someone give you a name?"

"When I was born?" the dragon asked, thinking hard.

"Yes," Minli said, again thinking that this dragon was very different from any dragon she had ever heard about. "What did they call you when you were born?"

 ## THE STORY OF THE DRAGON

When I was born, I remember two voices speaking.

"Master!" one voice said. "This is magnificent — the dragon is almost alive!"

"Add more water to the inkstone," another voice said. This voice was near my head, I felt the warm air of his breath. "And speak quietly. You will wake the dragon."

"I am sorry, Master," the first voice said in a more

subdued tone. "It is only that this painting is most amazing, even for such a skilled artist as you. This dragon painting will bring great honor to the village when we present it to the magistrate."

"Wasted on the magistrate," the master said under his breath, so softly that only I could hear. "A conceited, self-important man, who, when only the imperial family is allowed to use the image of a dragon, commissions one. Now that his son has married the king's daughter, Magistrate Tiger will do anything to flaunt his power and overstretch his authority. But this painting will buy his favor and free the village from his unfair taxes."

"What, Master?" the apprentice said.

"Nothing," the master said, "only that I have painted this dragon on the ground, not flying in the sky like all other dragons. Perhaps the magistrate will see how his wealth weighs him down."

"I doubt the magistrate will understand that meaning, Master," the apprentice said.

"True," the master said, "but the dragon should still please him. I will prepare for his visit. The painting is finished. Clean the brushes and take great care with my special inkstone. It is one of a kind, the only inkstone that was able to be made from a rock my master cut from a mountain far from here. He never told anyone which mountain, so we can never make another."

"Yes, Master," the apprentice said. "But the dragon . . ."

"Yes?" the master said.

"Is it finished?" the apprentice asked. "You have not painted the eyes."

"As a painting, it is finished," the master said. "Young apprentice, I still have much to teach you."

And I heard the voices and footsteps fade away. It was a strange feeling. I felt the warm light of the sun running over my skin, but my arms and legs were frozen. I could hear the wind rustling leaves in the trees and birds hopping on the ground but I saw nothing.

Time passed; I only knew because the air grew colder. I heard footsteps coming toward me, many of them, so I knew it was a whole procession of people.

"As you requested, Your Magnificence," a voice

said — I recognized it as the master's — "may I present this, which I humbly painted in tribute to the great magistrate's rule."

There was a silence as all gazed, I supposed, at me.

"Painter Chen," another voice said, in great awe, "this is indeed a great work."

"Thank you, Magistrate," the master said, "I am glad it pleases you. Then our agreement will be fulfilled?"

"Yes," said the voice, "the village will be free from taxation for the next year. And I will take the painting."

Even though I did not know exactly what was going on, I knew I did not want to belong to Magistrate Tiger. His voice had an undertone of cruelty and greed, even while he was expressing his pleasure. I tried to protest but my still lips uttered no sound. Then I was rolled up and all sound and feeling disappeared.

I do not know how long I was rolled up. It might have been a day or a month or a year. All I could do was wait. But finally I was unrolled and I felt a cold gust of air all over me. If I could have, I would have shivered.

"This painting is a masterpiece!" a voice said in surprise. Then it quickly turned oily and flattering. "As only fitting for your greatness."

"Yes," Magistrate Tiger said, "have it hung behind my chair."

"Yes, Magistrate," the voice said, and then hesitated and said, "How strange."

"What's strange?" the magistrate asked.

"Well," the voice said, "there are no eyes on this dragon. The painter must have forgotten."

"No eyes!" the magistrate boomed. "Painter Chen dared give me an unfinished painting! I will double tax his village for the next ten years!"

"Magistrate," a third voice said, one that seemed a little kinder, "it is only a minor flaw. If we just dotted in the eyes, the dragon would be finished."

"Hmm, yes," the magistrate said, obviously considering. "Bring me a paintbrush and ink."

I heard the servants shuffling and bringing the

paintbrush and ink. I felt the magistrate's hot, dry breath on my nose as he came close to me and felt the cold ink touch my eye and, suddenly, I could see! I saw the magistrate's fat face leering over me as he reached over and dotted in my other eye.

As sight came into both my eyes, a warm feeling filled me — like drinking hot tea on a cold day. I felt strength come into my arms and hands and legs and feet, and my neck and head stretched for the first time. All the loud yells I had wanted to make now came rushing out of my mouth and I gave a huge roar that made the magistrate fall over.

"It has come alive!" I heard him gasp, and I heard the servants screaming, "Dragon! It has come alive! Dragon!"

I knew this was my chance to free myself from Magistrate Tiger. I jumped from where I was and rushed over everyone, knocking down desks and chairs and columns. I saw the blue sky and green leaves through a window, went toward it, and simply crashed through the wall to get through. As I left, the building was falling down and all the people were yelling. "Dragon!" they screamed. "Dragon!"

I knew I had to leave as soon as possible, so I ran as fast as I could into the forest and left them far, far away. I have lived in the forest since then.

"So I think," the dragon said, "my name is Dragon. Because that is what everyone called me."

"Dragon," Minli repeated, and she tried not to smile. "Well, I guess it's a good enough name. It will be easy for me to remember."

The dragon nodded, pleased to have found himself a name.

"So you were born from a painting!" Minli said. "That explains why you are so different from the dragons my father told me about."

"Your father knew other dragons?" the dragon asked eagerly. "I have never seen another dragon. I always thought if I could fly, I would finally see another like me."

"Um, well," Minli said, "I don't think my father ever knew any dragons. He just told stories about them. Most people think dragons are just in stories. You are the only dragon I've ever met."

"Oh," the dragon said sadly, "and I am not even a real dragon."

All this time, Minli had been cutting the twine ropes. At that very moment, Minli cut the last rope and rubbed the dragon's arm. "You're the only dragon I've ever met in real life," she said, "and you feel real to me. So, I think you're a real dragon. Or, at least, real enough. Anyway, if we're going to Never-Ending Mountain together, let's at least be real friends."

"Yes," Dragon agreed, and they both smiled.

CHAPTER
12

The goldfish man turned around and smiled questioningly at Ma and Ba, who could do nothing but continue to stare. He was slender and small, which was perhaps why it was easy to mistake his footprints for Minli's. The dragging lines Ma had thought were from Minli's walking stick led to his cart, and the bowls of goldfish caught the sifting beams from the sun, slivering it into flashing sparkles of light. The goldfish man's eyes also flashed as he looked at Ma and Ba and their dust-covered clothes and haggard, tired faces.

"Can I help you?" he asked them.

"We were looking for our daughter," Ba stammered. "We are from the Village of Fruitless Mountain."

"You sold her a goldfish, and then," Ma sputtered, "and then she ran away to change our fortune."

"I see," the goldfish man said, and again, he looked at them — at Ma's tight, angry frown and Ba's careworn, worried face. "And you are going after her, to stop her?"

"Of course," Ba said. "We need to bring her home."

"Yes," Ma said. "She is acting crazy. Who knows what could happen to her?"

"She could succeed," the goldfish man said steadily. "She could find a way to change your fortune."

"She's trying to find Never-Ending Mountain!" Ma said. "Ask questions to the Old Man of the Moon! There is no way for her to succeed."

"Yes," Ba said, "it's impossible."

The goldfish man looked a third time at Ma and Ba, and this time they felt it. Under his gaze, Ma and Ba suddenly felt like freshly peeled oranges, and their words fell away from them. Inexplicably, they felt ashamed.

"Let me tell you a story," the goldfish man said.

THE STORY OF THE GOLDFISH MAN

My grandmother, Lao Lao, was a famous fortune-teller. People from faraway villages would line up at our home, asking for lucky dates for weddings and predictions for their children. If she was ever wrong, we never heard of it.

But a week before my nineteenth birthday, we heard her moaning in her room. When we rushed to her, we found her sitting on the floor with her fortune-telling sticks spread around her. To my surprise, as soon as I entered the room, her piercing eyes fixed upon me.

"You," she said, "you will die next week on your birthday."

It was as if she had exploded a firecracker in the room. My parents and aunts and cousins burst into exclamations and wails. "It is true, it is true," my grandmother insisted, "I have checked and rechecked over and over again. And the sticks always say the same. Next week, on his nineteenth birthday, he will die. That is his fortune."

I could not believe it. How could this be? But my belief in my grandmother was unshakable; if she said so, it must be true. I stood staring as my family created a storm around me. Finally I said with a mouth as dry as sand, "Lao Lao, isn't there anything I can do?"

"There is only one thing you can do," she said, "but it is doubtful it will work."

"I'll do it," I said.

"First," Lao Lao said, "we must get a bottle of the finest wine and make a box of sweets."

So Lao Lao went to the rich magistrate of the town and persuaded him to give her a bottle of his best wine. My mother and aunts hurried to the kitchen and prepared cakes, cookies, and sweetmeats with more care than ever before. Before the aromas of the delicacies were captured in our most ornate box, they floated in the air, causing all the neighborhood animals to whine at our door.

And then Lao Lao went to her room and began

to read her fortune sticks. When she came out, she gave me the box of sweets and bottle of wine and sat me down.

"Listen to me carefully," she said, "you must do exactly as I say. Tomorrow morning, you must walk north of the village. Do not stop until the moon begins to appear in the sky. When it does, you will see a mountain before you, and at the foot of the mountain you will see an old man reading a book. Open the box of sweets and bottle of wine and set them by him, but do not say a word unless he speaks to you first. This is the only chance we have to change your fortune."

So the next morning, I followed her instructions and it was as she'd said. I walked all day and when the sun finally withdrew from the sky, there was a vast mountain in front of me whose tip seemed to touch the moon. Sitting cross-legged at the bottom was an old man, reading a giant book. The light from the moon seemed to make him glow silver. I opened the bottle of wine and box of sweets and quietly laid them next to him. Then I sat and waited.

The old man didn't notice me and continued to

read. My mouth watered as the smell of the sweets drifted in the air, but I didn't move. And even though the old man was engrossed in his book, he must have smelled them as well because, without lifting his eyes from the page, he began to eat.

It was only when the bottle of wine was empty and he was eating the last cake that the old man lifted his head. He seemed surprised to see a half-eaten cake in his hand.

"I've been eating someone's food," he said to himself. He looked up and saw me sitting nearby. "You, boy, was this your food?"

"Yes," I said, and I came closer as he beckoned.

"Well," he said to me, "what are you doing here?"

I told the old man my story while he rubbed his beard. When I finished, he said nothing but began to turn pages in his book. Finally, he nodded.

"Yes, it's true," the old man said. "You are to live only nineteen years."

And he turned the book toward me and in the moonlight, I read my name on the page. Next to my name was the number nineteen.

"Please," I couldn't help asking, "isn't there any way to change it?"

"Change it?" the old man asked, surprised at the thought. "Change the Book of Fortune?"

"Yes." I nodded.

"Well," the old man said, stroking his beard, "I am indebted to you for having eaten your food."

He took a paintbrush from his robe and studied the page. "Hmm," he said to himself, "maybe if . . . no . . . perhaps . . . Ah! Yes, this is how it can be done!"

And with a simple flick from his brush, he changed the nineteen to ninety-nine. "Good," he said to me. "You now have many more years of life. Live them well."

Then, he closed his book, stood up, and began to walk up the mountain, leaving me staring behind him. I sat there until he disappeared from sight and then turned around and went home.

The next week, on my birthday, there was a terrible typhoon. The wind howled as it never had before and a tree fell right on top of the roof of our house and crashed into my room, narrowly missing me. If it had fallen just a bit more to one side, I would have been easily killed. But as I climbed out of the ruins of my room, I saw my grandmother's eyes staring into mine. Silently, she nodded. She did not need words to tell me what had happened. I knew my fortune had been changed.

"But for Minli to try to do that is different," Ba started. "She's trying to find Never-Ending Mountain . . . ask a question . . . she's just a small girl . . ."

"Perhaps," the goldfish man said, "you need to trust her."

"But," Ma said, "but what she wants is impossible."

"Impossible?" the goldfish man said. "Don't you see? Even fates written in the Book of Fortune can be changed. How can anything be impossible?"

Ma and Ba could find no words. His eyes and the hundreds of eyes of the goldfish behind him seemed to silently scold them. As they looked at the ground, the goldfish man shifted back his bag and turned toward his cart.

"Here, a gift," the goldfish man said, placing a bowl into Ba's shaking hands. The fish, the pale silver color of the moon, circled in the bowl. "Perhaps if you cannot trust that your daughter will find Never-Ending Mountain, you should trust that she will return home to you. Because that is not impossible. So, whether Minli brings it to you or not, I wish you good fortune."

And with a bow, the goldfish man walked away; his bowls of goldfish cast pieces of rainbows in the air, making him sparkle in the sun. Ma and Ba stood and watched him until he looked like a twinkling star in the distance.

CHAPTER
13

After cutting the dragon free, Minli's knife was dull and the skin on her fingers and toes was wrinkled from having been in the dragon's lake of tears for so long. She was also very thirsty.

The dragon offered to carry her to the freshwater stream. He knew the forest well. "You'll get there much faster," he said.

Minli was a little doubtful about riding the dragon. It was one thing to climb on top of him while he was half covered by water, but now on dry land she realized how large he really was. The dragon was long, as long as the street in front of Minli's house. If he stretched himself up on his arms and legs, he was as tall as a bird's nest in a tree, she realized. Even now, bending down for her, he was higher than her house.

But he bent his elbow for her like a step and with two hands, she boosted herself up and then climbed onto his back. The round ball on the dragon's head was the size of a small melon, just big enough for her to wrap two hands around, and she clutched it as the dragon began to move.

It was faster, but not much. The dragon was nimble, but his large body had to constantly maneuver around trees and rocks, so it was awkward going. The constant jerking made Minli feel like she was riding a huge water buffalo. As the dragon ducked underneath branches and swerved through trees, Minli understood why most dragons flew.

"Dragon," Minli asked suddenly, "how old are you?"

"Old?" the dragon said, and again it seemed a question he had never been asked. "I do not know."

"Well," Minli said, "how long have you been in this forest?"

The dragon thought hard. "A long time," he told her. "I remember when a bird flew from the sky and dropped a peach pit onto the ground. I watched that pit grow into a tree and the peaches fell from the tree and more trees grew from the pits of those peaches until it became the grove of peach trees that the monkeys have now taken over."

He is very old, Minli thought to herself, imagining the growth of the trees. *Dragon must have been in this forest for a hundred years.* And she felt a pang of pity as she imagined the dragon, alone, unable to fly, endlessly struggling between trees and branches.

After picking up her things and drinking at the freshwater stream, Minli climbed back onto the dragon's back. She soon fell asleep, her head on the dragon's ball and her hand holding her rice bowl. Noticing she was asleep, the dragon moved slowly and quietly, even when the water from Minli's compass splashed and trickled down his nose.

It was only when a loud shrieking filled the forest that Minli woke. It was such a wild and harsh noise that she bolted up, her eyes wide open in fear.

"Do not worry," the dragon told her, "it is just the monkeys."

And it was the monkeys — even though the sun was dimming, Minli could still see the monkeys clamoring in the trees. Even though Minli could not count that many of them, their screaming made it sound as if there were thousands.

"We are getting close to the peach trees," the dragon told Minli, "and they are getting angry."

"Stop here," Minli said. She climbed off the dragon's back and she could still see the monkeys through leaves and branches, their bared teeth flashing.

"Those peach trees are exactly the direction we want to go," Minli said. "We have to get past the monkeys."

"I could still force my way through, but the monkeys would attack you," Dragon said. "I am not sure if we could get you through unharmed. Listen to them."

And the monkeys continued to scream. Minli covered her ears with her hands, but she could still hear them. It seemed like they were screeching, "Get away from here!! Ours! Ours! All ours!"

"You're right," Minli told the dragon. "They are not going to let us through."

"But you said that is the way to the Old Man of the Moon," said the dragon. "Correct?"

Minli nodded. The monkeys' shrieks were starting to sound like hysterical laughter, getting louder and louder like a volcano about to erupt. She looked from side to side but the monkeys seemed to be everywhere. There was no way around them.

"Then," the dragon asked, "what are we going to do?"

CHAPTER
14

Minli and the dragon had sat in the clearing and made camp for the night. As the sun fell and the moon rose, the dragon showed her how he could make sparks by scratching his claws against a stone, and they built a small campfire. As Minli and the dragon made no moves to go farther into the forest, the monkeys had quieted down. But they still watched.

"There are plenty of peaches for all," Dragon said. "Those monkeys do not have to be so greedy."

"Really?" Minli asked.

"Yes," Dragon said, "the monkeys are so foolish. They just want more and more even when they do not need it. I have seen them refuse to let go of rotten mushrooms and fight over piles of mud."

At those words, Minli sat up and her eyes flashed with quick thinking. Piles of mud. Suddenly, Minli remembered the two children fighting over their piles of mud as she had left her village. Instead of going inside for dinner, the children had clung to their pretend dishes of dirt. They were so foolish. Could the monkeys be that foolish? They were too selfish for trading or bribes. But maybe they were so greedy that they could be foolish enough to be tricked? Maybe if she . . . "I'm going to make rice," Minli said abruptly.

"Oh," the dragon said, "you must be hungry. Too bad we cannot get you some peaches."

"It's not for me," Minli said, and she smiled mysteriously. "It's for the monkeys."

"The monkeys?" the dragon said. "Why? If you mean it as a gift or as a way to bribe them, it will not work. They will take it and eat it, but they still will not let you through."

"That is what I am expecting," Minli said as she filled her pot with water and uncooked rice. She was bursting to tell Dragon her idea, but wasn't sure how much the monkeys understood of their words. She looked at him with sparkling eyes, but he only stared back blankly.

"You are?" the dragon said. "I do not understand."

"Don't worry," Minli said, and with her eagerness she felt like the water she was boiling. "I think I know how we can pass the monkeys."

The dragon watched as Minli stirred the big pot of rice. Through the rising steam, he could see the beady eyes of all the monkeys glittering through the branches like hundreds of diamonds as they watched as well. "The monkeys are watching," he whispered to Minli.

"Good," she whispered back, "I hope they are."

When the rice was done, the pot was overflowing with snowy white rice. It was so heavy that to take it off the fire to cool she had to ask the dragon to move it for her. Minli had the dragon place it very close to the trees where the monkeys were watching. Then, Minli tied her fishnet over the rice and pot.

As Minli and the dragon turned away, they could hear the monkeys chattering.

"That fishnet will not stop the monkeys from taking the rice," the dragon said. "It is tightly woven, but their hands will probably fit through."

"I know," Minli said as she put out the fire. "Let's pretend that we think the rice is safe and we are letting it cool."

Though puzzled, the dragon nodded. They placed themselves a far distance from the rice, yet still within sight, put out the fire, and pretended to go to sleep.

But Minli could not help peeking. Though she tried to lie still, she was filled with excitement. Would her plan work? Would the monkeys take the rice?

In the bright light of the moon, the monkeys glanced slyly at them and stole over to the rice. The dragon was right; just as he'd said, the fishnet could not keep the monkeys from the rice. Their slender hands slid through the holes of the fishnet and each grabbed two big fistfuls of rice. But as the monkeys tried to carry the rice away, the net caught them. The holes in the net were large enough for their empty hands to fit through, but not large enough for their full fists!

The monkeys screamed and pulled; and Minli and the dragon no longer pretended to be asleep. They couldn't help laughing as they watched the monkeys struggling to punch the air and each other with their trapped fists.

Minli quickly packed her things and the monkeys screeched and shrieked as they passed. The heavy pot of rice shook as the monkeys fought violently to get free. But the fishnet was strong and well woven, and since the monkeys were too greedy to let go of the rice, Minli and the dragon entered the peach grove and continued through the forest.

CHAPTER
15

Ma and Ba sat in front of a small fire that Ba had built. Their disappointment at not having found Minli forced them to admit their exhaustion, and they had slept under the canopy of tree branches during the day, leaving their silver goldfish as a guardian.

By the time they'd awakened, it was late afternoon, but neither of them made any attempt to move. Neither spoke, but both knew they were unsure whether to go forward or go back.

While the sun burst into multicolored flames on the horizon, its last wave goodbye before surrendering to the night, Ma handed Ba a bowl of rice porridge. Neither of them spoke as they ate, both thinking about the goldfish man's words. Should they let Minli try to change their fortune? Should they stop looking and, like the goldfish man said, trust her? Ba sighed.

"Trying to find Minli is like trying to find the paper of happiness," Ba said aloud to himself.

"What paper of happiness?" a voice said. Ba looked sharply around. Who had said that? He looked at Ma, but she continued to stir her porridge, obviously unaware. Ba shook his head. Perhaps his weariness was making him imagine things.

"Tell the story, old man. She's listening," the voice spoke again. "She won't admit it, but she wants to hear it too."

Ba looked around again. It seemed like the voice was coming from . . . the goldfish? He looked closely at the bowl. Was it the firelight that made it glow like that? The fish stared back at him calmly, as if waiting. So Ba took a deep breath and began the story.

THE STORY OF THE PAPER OF HAPPINESS

O nce, a long, long time ago, a family grew famous for their happiness. It seemed odd that this would happen, but they were truly an unusual household. Even though aunts and uncles, cousins and grandchildren lived together, there was never a cross word or unhappy noise. All were polite and thoughtful to each other; even the chickens did not fight each other for feed. It was said even the babies were born smiling.

Stories of their happiness spread like seeds in the wind, sprouting and blooming everywhere, until finally even young Magistrate Tiger heard of them. Even though he had just begun his position (this was before his son was born), the bellowing, roaring magistrate was already called Magistrate Tiger. "Impossible," he scoffed. "The stories are exaggerated. No family can be that happy." But even so, he was curious and sent an emissary to the family to observe.

The emissary returned, awed. "Your Magnificence, it is just as the stories say," he said. "I observed the family for a full moon and not one sad or angry word was even whispered. The adults are loving and faithful, the children are gracious and respectful, and all honor the grandfather with an esteem that rivals the gods. Even the dogs do not bark, but wait patiently to be fed. The family circle is one of complete harmony."

"That's impossible," the magistrate said, astonished. But as he thought about it, the more he began to wonder. What was the secret that the family had? They must have some magical charm or hidden knowledge. And this began to irritate him. He began to covet the family's happiness. *I am the magistrate*, he thought. *If there is a secret to happiness, I should have it.*

So he called his emissary to him and presented him with an empty, heavily encrusted chest and a company of soldiers.

"Return to the family," Magistrate Tiger ordered, "and tell them that I want the secret of their happiness put in this box. If they do not do so, have the soldiers destroy their home."

The emissary did as he was told. When the troop of soldiers surrounded the house, the family looked fearful. But when the magistrate's demand was announced, the grandfather smiled.

"That is easy enough," he said, and he had the trunk brought into the house and returned in moments. "It is done. I've put the secret of our happiness inside the box," he said, "and you may take it. We hope it serves our magistrate well."

The emissary was slightly surprised at the ease of his task, but could find no objection, so he turned the soldiers and the box around and began to travel back to the palace.

The emissary knew the magistrate would be impatient for his return, so the soldiers marched through the night, with only the light of the moon to guide them. The treasure box, lying on a platform carried by four men, seemed to glow.

However, as the ground grew rocky and steep, a sudden wind blew — like the mountain itself was yawning. One of the soldiers stumbled in the rising dust, and the box crashed to the ground. The lid of the box flew off and, like a freed butterfly, a single sheet of paper fluttered out.

"Get it!" the emissary shouted at the soldiers. "Don't lose the secret!"

But despite his yells, the paper seemed to be able to escape the soldiers' flailing arms. One soldier almost caught it, his very fingertips touching the page, but another sudden wind burst through the air and stole it away. Silently, the emissary and the soldiers watched the paper lift higher and higher in the night sky, until it overlapped the moon and disappeared.

The emissary had no choice but to return to the palace with an empty box. As he relayed the story, Magistrate Tiger, not surprisingly, was enraged.

"You lost it! It was a paper?" the magistrate roared. "What was on it?"

"Your Magnificence" — the emissary trembled — "as I felt the secret was for your eyes only, I did not read the paper before it was lost. However, as it was in the air, all could see that there was a single line of words on it."

"What did the line say?" the magistrate demanded.

"I don't know, Magistrate," the emissary said, "but there was one soldier who almost caught it and was closest to it. Perhaps he was able to read the line."

So the soldier was called in, and very humbly did he bow. He was little more than a boy and had only recently joined the magistrate's army from a small, poor, faraway village.

"You," the magistrate said, "you were the only soldier close enough to the paper to read the line. What did it say?"

The boy flushed and his head touched the floor as he bowed again.

"Great Magistrate, I am your poor servant," he said. "I was close enough to see the line on the page . . . however, I cannot read. I do not know what the line said."

Magistrate Tiger scowled with irritation and the emissary and the soldier shivered.

"I . . . I did notice something," the soldier said.

"What?" the magistrate demanded.

"There was only one character on the page," the soldier said. "The line was one word written over and over again, many times."

"One word?" the magistrate snarled, and his anger seemed to burn deep in his eyes. "One word is the secret to happiness? It was a trick! The family must have thought they could deceive me! Emissary, gather all of my troops. I, personally, will get the secret of happiness and punish that family of lowly dogs!"

So, the next day, with Magistrate Tiger and his entire army prepared for destruction, the emissary led the way to the home of the happy family. But when they arrived, nothing was there! No house, no chickens or sheep, no family! Instead, there was only a flat plain, as if the whole home had been scooped from the earth.

Magistrate Tiger scowled at the blank ground with rage and vowed to punish the family for their disrespect. But while he glared, the wind blew and covered him with a grayish green dust. As he stood like a green powdered statue, he felt as if the sky were laughing at him.

"So, I think Minli, like the secret word and the paper of happiness," Ba said, "is not meant to be found." He glanced at Ma and while she did not meet his gaze, she made no objection either.

"And, tomorrow," Ba continued, gently, "we should return and wait for her to come home."

Again, Ma said nothing but barely, perhaps only because he was looking for it, she nodded. Ba nodded back at her and quietly took some rice and dropped it into the fishbowl.

CHAPTER
16

Feasting on juicy peaches, Minli and the dragon walked through the woods for many days. At night, when the dragon slept, Minli missed Ma and Ba. "But this is for our fortune, so they don't have to work so hard anymore," Minli told herself when she thought about the worry they must have been feeling. "When I get back, Ba can rest and Ma will never have to sigh again. They'll see." But the lonely moon never seemed to gaze comfortably down at her.

One day Minli and the dragon came upon a body of water. In the distance, they saw the woods continue. As the compass pointed across the water, the dragon swam the inlet with Minli riding his back.

"How far do we go before we get to Never-Ending Mountain?" the dragon asked.

"Well," Minli said slowly, "the fish said to go west until I reached the City of Bright Moonlight. Once there, I'm supposed to find the Guardian of the City."

"The Guardian?" Dragon said. "Who is that?"

"I'm not sure," Minli said. "The king of the city, I guess. Once I find him, I'm supposed to ask for the borrowed line, which, according to the fish, is something I'll need for Never-Ending Mountain."

"The borrowed line?" the dragon asked. "What is that?"

"I don't know," Minli said. "The fish didn't tell me."

"You did not ask?" The dragon almost stopped swimming in surprise.

"I didn't want to delay her," Minli said. "She was in a rush."

The dragon shook his head and opened his mouth to say something when they both heard a strange sound next to them in the water.

"Aunt Jin! Aunt Jin!" a voice said. "Is it you? You came back like you said!"

Dragon and Minli looked in the water and saw a large orange fish with a black fin swimming next to them. It looked a lot like Minli's goldfish but larger.

"I think you have me mixed up with someone else," Minli said to the fish.

"I was speaking to the dragon," the fish said, "but you must not be Aunt Jin either."

"Well" — the dragon looked down at the fish with a wry smile — "either one of us would be a very strange relative to you, Fish. Why did you think I was your aunt?"

"Because Aunt Jin always said she would come back to show us that the Dragon Gate was real," the fish said.

"What do you mean?" Minli asked. "Dragon Gate? What's that?"

THE STORY OF THE DRAGON GATE

Even though no fish has seen the Dragon Gate, we all know about it. Perhaps the story was told to us through the waves of water while we were eggs or whispered to us by the roots of the lotus flowers.

We all know that somewhere in one of the rivers of the land, there is a great and powerful waterfall; it is so high and so vast that it is as if water were gushing from a cut in the heavens. At the top of that waterfall, beyond anyone's view, is the Dragon Gate.

The Dragon Gate is an entryway to the sky. It is old, so old that it's possible that the gray stone columns grew from the mountain it stands on. Wind and time have worn and smoothed the gate's tiered placards that barely show the old carvings of the five colored clouds of heaven.

Above the placards are the tiled arches the same color as the misty sky. Nine hundred and ninety-nine small dragon ornaments perch on the ridges of those tiled roofs. Each one is intricately formed to the smallest detail and, even weathered as they are, the black pearl eyes still flash with a mysterious power. That is because these dragons are not mere decoration — they hold the secret to the Dragon Gate.

For if ever a fish is able to swim up the waterfall and pass through the gate, the dragons will shake with power. As the fish goes through, its spirit enters the gate and bursts out of one of the ornaments — changing the fish into the form of a flying dragon!

"So the Dragon Gate transforms fish into dragons, a wish many of us hold deep in our hearts," the fish finished. "None know who first told the story, or if it is even a story at all. But Aunt Jin was determined to find out. She said she was going to search all the rivers of the land for it and if she found it she'd come back here as a dragon, to show us. That's why I thought you might be her."

"Did your aunt look like you?" Minli asked, "Orange with a black fin?"

"Yes," the fish said, "but much smaller, the size of a copper coin."

"It doesn't seem likely that a fish that small could swim up a waterfall," Dragon said. "Even if she does find the right river, she might not be able to get to the gate."

"If there is a gate, Aunt Jin will find a way through it," the fish said. "She's very wise. If you knew her, you'd understand."

"Maybe I do know her," Minli said softly, thinking hard about the goldfish she'd set free. Could it be that her goldfish, who had swum all the rivers except one, had been Jin searching for the Dragon Gate?

"If you are not Aunt Jin," the fish said to the dragon, interrupting Minli's thoughts, "why are you swimming across the river? Why don't you just fly?"

"He can't fly," Minli answered for the dragon, when she saw his discomfort. "We are going to go see the Old Man of the Moon to ask him how to change that. But we have to cross the river to get to the City of Bright Moonlight first."

"Old Man of the Moon?" the fish said. "Good luck! Finding him will be harder than finding the Dragon Gate!"

Minli and the dragon looked at each other and shrugged.

"But the City of Bright Moonlight is just past the forest, over there," the fish continued. "Swim over to this side and you can see it in the distance."

And, just as the fish said, Minli and the dragon saw the city. An enormous wall, like a giant patchwork curtain of stone, surrounded the thousands of houses of the city. And almost glowing with the splendor of its red columns and golden top, a palace stood up over the clusters of buildings in the far center — like a glorious boat floating above the waves of the scalloped rooftop tiles. Even from a distance, the city looked majestic.

"If you are stopping at the City of Bright Moonlight," the fish continued, "I think Dragon here should probably try to stay hidden. People of Bright Moonlight might be shocked to see a real dragon. The last dragon sighted was about a hundred years ago — and it destroyed the king's father's palace in a city in the East. They might not take too kindly to you."

"That is good to know," Minli said. "It might be better if I go into the city by myself."

"Yes," the dragon agreed, "I can hide at the edge of the forest and wait for you."

"They close the wall at night," the fish said, "so if you are in the city at night, you have to stay until morning."

"Do not worry," Dragon said to Minli, "I will wait."

"Well, you're almost to land," the fish said, "so I'll leave you. If you ever see another dragon, find out if it's my Aunt Jin. Hope you get to meet the Old Man of the Moon. Good luck!"

Minli and the dragon watched the fish swim away. Then they made their way to the land and the City of Bright Moonlight.

CHAPTER

17

Minli gulped as she walked toward the gray stone wall of the city. As she passed the two stone lions marking the entrance, she glanced behind her. Even though she only saw the trees and shadows, she knew the dragon was hidden there. Quickly, she pushed through the doors of the gate, leaving the forest and the dragon behind her.

As the gate closed, Minli stared. The streets were crowded and bustling; the city seemed to be bubbling with people like boiling rice. Vendors selling fruit and shoes called out their wares while people rushed past —

some pushing wheelbarrows or balancing baskets on their shoulders. A large muddy water buffalo, led by a boy perhaps a year or two older than Minli, wandered through and was ignored as a commonplace occurrence.

"Watch out, Little Mouse," a gruff man said behind her, his baskets of cabbages driving her into the crowd. As she was shoved and pushed, Minli grabbed the arm of the boy with the water buffalo.

"Hi," she said. "If I want to see the king, where do I go?"

"The king?" The boy looked at her in surprise. "You'd have to go to the palace."

"How do I get to the palace?" Minli asked.

"Just follow the black stones," the boy said, pointing at the road paved with polished bricks. "They'll lead you to the City."

"Wait," Minli said, "isn't this the City? The palace is in another city?"

"You must not be from around here," the boy laughed. "The City of Bright Moonlight is divided into two. This is the Outer City, where anyone can live and travel. The Inner City is where the palace is, where the king and officials live. You have to have permission to go into the Inner City. If you don't, you're not going to be able to see the king or the palace. There are thousands of guards protecting the Inner City; they won't let anyone through without permission."

"I'll find a way," Minli said, confidently. "Thanks." And she let go of the boy's arm and headed toward the black road.

However, as Minli got closer to the Inner City, she realized the boy was right. The red walls of the Inner City loomed tall and forbidding, and every gold-studded gate door was guarded by at least two soldiers, their silver armor reflecting in the hot sun. It would be a daunting task just to enter the Inner City, much less find the palace and the king.

"But I must," Minli said to herself. Regardless, the guards' faces were stern and hard, and she quaked inside. *If I ask to go in,* Minli thought as she hung back amongst the fruit stands and fish vendors, *they'll ignore me or force me away with their swords. And either way, I won't be able to see the king. What should I do?*

"Not as easy as you thought, huh?" a voice said next to

her. Minli turned and saw the buffalo boy standing next to her.

Minli gave him a wry look. *Boys,* she thought to herself, *always thinking they know everything.* Still, she had to admit, he was right. She had no idea how she would see the king. "They must let people into the Inner City sometimes," Minli said.

"They do," the boy said. "Once a year at the Moon Festival, they open the gates to everyone."

"When's the Moon Festival?" Minli asked.

"Already happened," the boy said. "You'll have to wait until next year."

Minli bit her lip in frustration. What was she going to do?

"I don't know why you want to go in there so badly," the boy said. "The buildings and clothes are nicer, but the people! A bunch of puffed-up frogs! At the Moon Festival one of the stable men wanted to order me around and thought he could trick me into thinking he was the king. But when I asked why he wasn't wearing a golden dragon, he knew his prank wasn't going to work. Did he think I was stupid? Everyone knows a golden dragon is always and only worn by kings and the emperor. The people in there think we're a bunch of dumb oxen."

The buffalo beside the boy gave a snort at that. "Sorry," the boy said, patting the buffalo on the nose, "you know I didn't mean that."

But by this time, the Inner City guards had seen them lingering by the gate.

"You there, kids," one of them barked. "Move along!"

"Come on," the boy said, tugging Minli's sleeve. "Let's go."

Minli followed him and the buffalo. "Where are you going?" she asked him.

"I'm going home," he said. "You can come too, if you want."

And since Minli had no place else to go, she did.

CHAPTER
18

Minli followed the boy through the maze of streets and alleyways for what seemed like a long time. If it wasn't for the big buffalo that was always in view, Minli would've easily lost him many times. "Not too far now," the boy said to her.

Minli realized that the boy lived very far from the Inner City. The road was no longer stone, but dirt. Even from a distance, she could see that the Outer City wall was cracked and broken. "I live over here," the boy said, pointing. And Minli looked down a muddy path that led to a shabby, rickety hut that looked as if the first strong wind would blow it away.

The boy brought the buffalo right into the hut, and Minli went in after. She looked around the small, meager home. The only furnishings Minli could see were two wooden crates and a rough stool. On one side of the hut a crude metal grate stood in the fireplace with a well-worn pot on it. The other half of the hut was divided into two piles of dry grass. Minli watched as the buffalo went directly to one pile and lay down. The boy gave it an affectionate slap on the side and dragged the rough wooden stool across the floor to her.

"Here, have a seat," he said as he sprawled onto the other pile of grass, "and tell me why you want to go to the palace so much."

"It's not the palace," Minli said as she sat on the stool, "I want to see the king." And she told the buffalo boy the whole story. She saw his face wrinkle with disbelief when she talked about the fish and he shook his head when she told about the dragon, but he didn't interrupt once.

"I don't know how you are going to see the king," the boy told her when she finished. "Even if you do see him, I doubt you'll be able to ask for a borrowed line, especially when you don't even know what it is!"

"But I have to," Minli said. "There must be a way."

"Well, I always think better after I've eaten," the boy said, and he stood up and opened one of the crates. "Let's have dinner."

While he fried the plain bamboo shoots in the pot over the fireplace, Minli looked around the bare room.

"Do you live by yourself?" she asked.

"Uh-huh." The boy nodded. "My parents died four years ago. Ever since then, it's been me and the buffalo."

He spoke almost carelessly, without anger or self-pity. Suddenly, Minli thought about her own home — the wood floor always swept by Ma, the extra blanket Ba put over her when the wind blew cold — and she felt a strange tightness in her throat.

The boy finished cooking and pushed the cooked bamboo, like thinly sliced pieces of yellow wood, onto a plate. He only had one plate so he set it on the stool next to the three peaches Minli had left, and both sat cross-legged on the ground. She took out her chopsticks (he only had one pair of those as well) and each picked and ate with the stool as a table and the single plate between them.

"You don't have any aunts or uncles?" Minli asked. "Other family or friends?"

"Well," the boy said, tossed a peach to the buffalo, and then hesitated. "I do have one friend." And Minli was surprised to see his face change unexpectedly. The sharpness of his expression softened like a flower blossoming, his small smile gentle.

"Who is it?" Minli asked.

THE STORY OF THE BUFFALO BOY'S FRIEND

Sometimes, during the hot summer days, there is not enough water for my buffalo, so I like to take him out of the city into the surrounding forest to drink in the stream there. One day, I brought him to the forest and he kept pulling and pushing me away from the stream. No matter what I did, he refused to go in my direction. So finally, I just let him lead the way.

And he brought me to a part of the forest I had never seen before, a part I don't think anyone from the city has ever seen before. The trees seemed to reach the clouds, the green grass felt like a silk blanket, and there was a lake of clear water, so pure and clean it looked as if it were a piece of the sky. But the most beautiful things there were the seven girls swimming in it.

But when the girls saw me and the buffalo come through the trees, they screamed. They jumped out of the water, grabbed their robes, and ran away. They moved so quickly, it seemed like they had all disappeared into the sky.

All except for one, that is. One girl stayed in the water and stared at me with scared eyes. Her hair floated around her like a midnight halo and her white face looked like a star in the sky.

"Hello?" I said.

"Your . . . your buffalo," she said, and her voice was like flute notes in the air, "he's sitting on my clothes!"

"Oh," I said, and I quickly pushed him over. On the ground, crushed and a little muddy, was a blue silk dress. As I lifted it, the softness made me ashamed of my rough hands. "Here," I said, bringing the dress to the edge of the lake.

She looked at me, hesitating. "I won't look," I said, and I placed the dress on the ground and walked a bit away, with my back turned. I heard her slip out of the water and heard the rustle of silk as she put on her clothes.

"Thank you," she said. "You can turn around now."

And when I turned around, a girl was smiling at me. She was my age but she was prettier than any girl I had ever seen before. Even paintings of princesses were ugly compared to her.

"I didn't mean to scare you," I said. "My buffalo was just thirsty."

"I guess so," she said, and she laughed like tinkling bells as we watched my big, lumbering buffalo make his way to the water. "I can't believe my sisters just left me like that! I'm the youngest too — they're supposed to watch me. But I'm glad they didn't because now I can talk to you. Tell me all about you! Does your buffalo go with you everywhere?"

And just like that, we became good friends. She wanted to know everything about me and wasn't snobbish or anything. In fact, a lot of the time she sighed and said she wished she had my freedom.

"I have to go before they miss me." She sighed. "I wish I could stay here. Where I live, I'm not allowed to do anything. There's always someone watching, telling me what to do. And it's kind of lonely."

"Well, visit me," I told her. "We can have lots of fun together."

"I'll try," she promised.

And she kept her promise. Like she said, it was hard for her to get away, but every night on the full moon when she visits her grandfather, she stops here. Sometimes she can only stay for a little while, sometimes she can stay for hours. Whenever I see her, we laugh enough to last for the month. She's my best friend, and someday when we're old enough I'm going to talk her into staying here forever.

"And she should be coming tonight," the buffalo boy said, and his smile was bright and broad.

"Oh, can I meet her?" Minli said. It was funny how the buffalo boy's whole manner changed when he talked about her — his vaguely mocking attitude and tough expression washed away and he lit up like a lantern. She was glad the boy had someone in his life other than the buffalo.

The boy looked troubled. "She's really shy around other people," he said. "And I think she's afraid if anyone sees her, her family might find out that she stops here instead of going straight to her grandfather's. They're really strict with her."

"I won't bother her, then," Minli said. "Do you want me to leave?"

"No, you can just stay with the buffalo," he said. "She

told me last time that this visit would have to be fast anyway. She was behind on her work, so they will expect her back quickly."

"Work?" Minli asked. "What does she do?"

"She weaves and spins thread," the boy said. "That's what she brings to her grandfather when she visits — thread that she spins. Hey, I know! I'll ask her how you can see the king! She'll know."

"How will a weaving girl know about the king?" Minli asked. "Does she live in the Inner City?"

"No, she lives far away," the boy said vaguely, "but she knows a lot of things."

Minli shrugged. It didn't seem likely to her that a friend of the buffalo boy would know how she could see the king, but as she didn't have any ideas of her own, she would hope.

CHAPTER
19

Minli started awake as she heard the scraping of the door against the dirt. The moonlight streamed in from the window, lighting the bare hut. The boy had given her his pile of grass to sleep on and joined the buffalo, using some of its grass as a pillow. But as the buffalo snored loudly, Minli could see the bowl-shaped hollow in the hay was empty. "I wonder where he went?" Minli said, and she found herself thinking of Ma and Ba and Dragon all waiting for her. Suddenly the room seemed to ache with loneliness.

"The boy must be meeting his friend," Minli realized, and unable to control her curiosity, she crept to the window to peek.

Yes, the friend was there. Minli was startled when she saw her. Even with the buffalo boy blocking most of her view, Minli could see his friend was beautiful, even more beautiful than he had described her. She seemed to glow like a pearl in the moonlight and her deep blue silk dress seemed to be the same color as the sky. The bag she held in her graceful hand seemed to be made out of the same silk, but the silver thread embroidered on it made it look as if it were made from a piece of the star-scattered sky. Everything about her seemed finer and more delicate than the average person. There was definitely something unusual about the buffalo boy's friend.

Minli watched her laugh and then listen intently as the buffalo boy spoke. He gestured to the house and Minli ducked down just out of sight as the friend glanced toward her. *He must be asking her about how I can see the king,* Minli thought.

As soon as she dared, Minli peeked again out the

window. The buffalo boy's friend had her eyes closed toward the sky, as if listening to the wind. Then she looked at the buffalo boy and spoke. He nodded and the girl smiled at what Minli imagined was the buffalo boy's enthusiastic thanks.

Minli sat down on the wooden stool. "She knows a lot of things," the buffalo boy had said about his friend. After seeing her, Minli was ready to believe it. "But who is she?" Minli asked aloud.

And just then the buffalo boy came back inside. "Oh, you're awake," he said when he saw Minli. As much as he tried he couldn't hide the leftover smiles and laughter from his visit; his eyes sparkled as he sprawled himself out on the bed of grass. "I talked to my friend. She said that the king might be at the Market of Green Abundance to-morrow morning, but you are going to have to find him yourself."

"Really?" Minli said. "How does she know?"

The boy shrugged.

"You didn't ask?" Minli asked. "Don't you think it's mysterious that you only see her once in a while? And you never visit her, she only visits you? And that she knows things like where the king might be tomorrow? Who is she, really?"

"She's my friend," the boy said simply. "That's who she is and that's enough for me."

As Minli looked at the buffalo boy, aglow with happiness against his poor surroundings, she saw it was enough for him. More than enough, as the smile that kept curling up on his face told her. Minli's questions fell from her as she realized there was nothing else to say.

CHAPTER
20

Ma and Ba walked quietly through the forest. Their steps made a rhythm to the music of forest noises. Ba's arms ached from carrying the goldfish bowl, but he said nothing.

"I can carry the goldfish if you are tired," Ma said.

Ba opened his mouth to protest when he heard, "Let her, old man. It's her way of saying she's not angry anymore."

Ba closed his mouth and looked at the fishbowl and then at Ma. She stood, waiting, clearly ignorant of the fish's words. He handed the bowl to Ma. "If it gets heavy, I can take it back," he said.

"We can take turns," Ma said, nodding.

Ma was carrying the fishbowl when the night fell and they came back home to the village. The neighbors saw their return and all crowded around as if they were selling good luck. "Did you find Minli?" they asked. "Where is she? Where did you get a goldfish?"

Both Ma and Ba shook their heads over and over again. "No," they said, "we didn't find her. We don't know where she is. The goldfish is from the goldfish peddler. We followed his footprints thinking they were Minli's."

"And we decided," Ba finally said, "to come back and wait. After she finds Never-Ending Mountain, Minli will come home."

"Wait for her!" one of the neighbors said. "How can you let your daughter search for Never-Ending Mountain? You are just as lost as her!"

"We tried to find her, but now we do not know where to look. So, we will wait," Ba said, and then glanced at Ma, who, though her lips tightened at the neighbors' words, did not disagree. "We trust Minli. She will come home."

And then Ma and Ba went into their house, leaving the sea of shaking heads behind them. Ma placed the goldfish bowl on the table and quietly began making dinner. A soft breeze seemed to blow in the moonlight, spilling it through the open window and lighting the bowl like a lantern. Ba looked at Ma cautiously; her face looked weary but the gentle wind that rippled the bowl's water seemed to smooth the creases of her face. And, when the cloud-white rice was finished, Ma took her chopsticks and fed the fish from her bowl.

CHAPTER
21

Minli and the buffalo boy pushed through the crowd as the sun burned the tops of their heads. Minli, used to the spare harvests of her village, couldn't help gaping at the tall mounds of food for sale at the Market of Green Abundance. The street and open courtyard were filled with umbrella-covered stands and stalls, flaunting jade-colored cabbages, curled cucumbers, purple eggplants, and tangy oranges. Glossy sugared hawthorne berries, like rubies on a stick, made Minli's mouth water.

"I don't see the king anywhere," Minli said.

"Well, maybe he's not here yet," the buffalo boy said.

"I don't know if I'll find him here," Minli said. Now, in the daylight, the buffalo boy's friend didn't seem as extraordinary. "What would the king be doing at a street market anyway?"

"She said he'd be here, so he will," the buffalo boy said, his mouth making a stubborn line.

"Hey! Get away from that!" a vendor yelled as the buffalo attempted to eat frosty green lettuce. The buffalo boy quickly pulled him away. "Get your buffalo out of here!" the vendor shouted, as red-faced as the radishes he was selling.

"I better take him away," the buffalo boy said, pulling the buffalo's head away from the arrays of tempting food. "He's hungry, I should take him to pasture."

"I'll stay here," Minli said. "You don't need to look for the king with me."

"Okay," the boy said. "If you need a place to stay tonight, you know where my hut is. If not, maybe I'll see you around! Good luck!"

"Thanks," Minli said, but as he carelessly waved goodbye, she realized that she might not see him again.

Before he disappeared from sight, she grabbed the last coin out of her bag, and ran to him. "Wait," Minli said. "Here, take this."

"No," the boy laughed, "I don't need that, you keep it."

"But . . . ," Minli started, but he had already turned around. "Goodbye!" she heard him call, and the buffalo snorted a farewell as well. Minli smiled wryly to herself.

Now what? Minli thought as she wandered past stalls, weaving around merchants and customers. *How am I supposed to find the king here?*

"Please, spare a piece of fruit for an old man," a voice creaked. Minli turned around and saw a wrinkled, poor man begging at a peach stand. He was dirty and bent and his clothes looked as if they were made from rags used to wash floors. "Please," he begged the peach vendor, "I'm so thirsty. One small peach, your smallest?"

"Go away, old man," the fat vendor said. "No money, no peach."

"Please," the beggar said again, weakly. "Pity a tired, old man."

"Get away from here, you worthless beggar!" the vendor spat out. "Or I'll call the guards on you."

The vendor's loud voice had attracted attention from passersby, and a small crowd began to form in front of the peach stand.

"It's disgraceful to treat an old man like that," someone murmured. "Just give him a peach."

"All of you are so generous with *my* property." The vendor glared at the crowd. "If you care so much, *buy* him a peach."

As Minli watched the beggar's hands outstretched and shaking with hunger, she felt a sharp pang inside her. It reminded her of Ba, reaching out with his last chopstickful of rice for her fish. The copper coin she had offered to the buffalo boy was warm in her hand. She could almost feel her heart beating against its round edges.

"Here," she said, handing the vendor the coin. Then she picked the largest peach on the stand and handed it to the old man. He bowed to her gratefully and eagerly ate the peach. Forgetting about the Inner City and the Palace for the moment, Minli watched him. In fact, as if under a spell, the whole crowd stood and watched him swallow the fruit until he held a peach pit in his hand.

"Thank you," the beggar said in a much stronger voice,

and he bowed to the onlooking people. "The peach was so delicious, I wish for all of you to be able to taste it. If you would humor an old man and stay a little while, I'll share my good fortune."

The old man took a small stick out of his pocket and bent down. In the dirt next to the black bricks, he dug a small hole and planted his peach pit. He stuck his stick upright in the little mound and then asked for water. Minli, now completely fascinated, took out her water jug and handed it to him. As he poured water onto his stick, it trembled, and — was she imagining it? — it seemed to grow.

And it *was* growing. The stick grew higher and higher and thicker and thicker, until it was the width of Minli's arm. When she could no longer see the top of it, pink flowers and branches began to blossom out of it. As the sweet scent of the flowers filled the air, Minli realized the stick had become a peach tree. The crowd of people seemed to realize this too as they all gaped at it open-mouthed. Even the stingy vendor left his fruit stand to stare at it in awe.

Like pink snow, the petals fell from the tree and made

a soft carpet on the dirt. Green leaves sprouted and, as they cascaded over the branches, pale moon-colored balls like pearls developed. Almost as if they were small balloons being blown with air, they grew into round fruit, blushing pink and red as they developed. Soon, the tree was heavy with them and the air was full of the enchanting smell of ripe peaches. Children gathered around and stared longingly at the luscious fruit while the adults gulped with their mouths watering.

Finally the old man reached up, plucked a peach from the tree, and handed it to one of the people in the crowd. "Please," he said, waving his hand, "help yourself."

The crowd needed no other urging. Young children climbed the tree and passed down the fruit, while the taller adults simply stretched and grabbed. A boy with a tired horse climbed onto its back to reach an especially red peach that called him. Before long, everyone's mouths were full of soft, sweet peach flesh and groans of delight. Even the peach vendor, his stand forgotten, stood under the tree with his eyes closed contentedly and peach juice dribbling out of his mouth.

Minli, however, didn't join in the feast of peaches. *If I*

hadn't been eating peaches all the way to the city, Minli said to herself, *I'd be the first one climbing the tree.* But as she was slightly tired of peaches, Minli saw what no one else did. She noticed that every time someone plucked a peach from the tree, a peach from the fruit stand disappeared.

The beggar is using the vendor's peaches for his tree! Minli laughed to herself as she glanced at him through the fruit-eating crowd. He was watching with an amused look, and suddenly Minli saw that the beggar wasn't really that old at all. "He must be a magician. Maybe he can help me get into the Inner City."

Minli edged toward him. As she weaved her way to him, the last peach was picked from the tree and the leaves and branches began to disappear. The tree trunk seemed to shrivel into itself and it grew thinner and shorter. The crowd had finished their peaches and the ground was littered with peach pits. When Minli finally reached the beggar, the tiny twig of the tree vanished underneath the pile of peach pits and the beggar was turning to leave.

"Wait!" Minli said, and grabbed his arm. However, as Minli took hold of his sleeve, it pulled back and a glint of gold shone. Hastily, the beggar pushed back his sleeve, but the quick glance was enough for Minli to see that he wore a gold bracelet in the shape of a dragon. They stared at each other, as Minli's quick-thinking mind somersaulted. *Only the imperial family is allowed to use the image of a dragon,* Dragon had said. *Everyone knows a golden dragon is always and only worn by kings,* said the buffalo boy. The words flashed in her mind and Minli could scarcely breathe.

"You're wearing a dragon," Minli gasped. "Only the . . . is allowed to wear a golden dragon . . . you must be . . . you must be . . ."

"Where's that beggar?!" a loud angry shout cut through the chaos. Minli recognized the vendor's voice. "He stole my peaches! I'll get him!"

Quickly, the beggar shook off Minli from his arm and began to run. She stared in shock as she finished her sentence. "You must be," Minli whispered to the ragged, disappearing figure, "the king!"

CHAPTER
22

Minli shook herself from her shock. "The king!" Minli said. "I can't lose him now!" And in a panic, she began to run after the tattered figure.

And it was quite a chase, or it would've been if the beggar had realized he was being followed. He wove in and out, around people and bins of rice, each step taking them closer to the unused areas of the city. Behind a pile of discarded baskets, Minli thought she had lost him but luckily the gray sleeve of his loose jacket waved at her, and she saw him round the walled corner of the Inner City.

As an abandoned wagon hid her from his view, she saw him push against a portion of the wall. With a slow groan, the wall moved!

"It's a secret door to the Inner City!" Minli gasped, and she was able to reach it just before it closed completely. With both hands she pressed hard against it and the door pushed open.

And like a lid of a jewelry box, the door opened into a landscape of radiant colors. The bamboo, pine, and plum leaves seemed to shine in the sun as if carved from emeralds, and the accents of the pink and red flowers were like nestled rubies. Steps away from her feet, Minli could see a patterned pathway made of water-worn pebbles. The central jade green lake mirrored the arching tiled roofs of the pavilions and the rough beauty of large weathered rock sculptures. A winding covered walkway lifted up from the cloudy water like a lotus flower. It could only be the Palace Garden.

But Minli barely noticed this. Instead she stood with large eyes, staring at the figure in front of her. The beggar was wiping his face with a delicate white cloth and Minli saw again that he was not an old man at all. In fact, he was younger than Ba — the gray of his hair was wiped away with the cloth as well — and his beard and head were as glossy black as Minli's. His gray rags had been cast off in a pile next to him and he was clothed in a bright yellow silk, the color of the sun. Intricate dragons and multicolored clouds that matched the designs of the gold bracelet he wore were embroidered on his robes and glittered in the light. There was no doubt now that he was the king.

Then, the king turned around and saw her. At his glance, Minli shrank to the ground in a humble kowtow.

"Your Majesty," Minli breathed, and her knees could feel the thumping of her heart in her chest.

"Caught!" Minli heard him say, and she peeked up to see the king looking at her with the same amused expression he'd had as a beggar watching the people eat the peaches. He shook his head at her. With his eyes twinkling at her, he could've been the young father of one of her village friends. "And by you," he said, "my little benefactor. I knew you were a clever one."

"Your Majesty! Your Majesty!" a chorus of voices came through the air toward them, and Minli could see a parade of servants in the distance running across the zig-zagged bridge.

"Well, you mustn't be caught by them!" the king said to Minli. "Then they would find out all about my little adventures and then where will I be?" And he pulled Minli up to her feet and pushed her behind one of the giant gnarled stone carvings, kicking his rags over her. "Quickly, quickly!" he said. "And don't say a word. I command you not to say a word or to come out until I say so."

Minli clutched the rough stone and made herself as small as possible. Hundreds of footsteps were approaching, like falling rain from a thunderstorm.

"What is this?" the king demanded. "Has war been declared on the city?"

"Your Majesty," an out-of-breath voice said, "we have been searching for you . . ."

"Searching for me?" the king said. "I have been here in the garden for hours."

"We . . . we must have missed you," the voice stuttered. "None could find you . . . the guards had not seen you and we feared . . ."

"You feared the King of the City of Bright Moonlight

had been spirited away?" The king laughed. "Not this time, Counselor Chu. However, I do feel the wish to commune with the moon tonight."

"Your Majesty?" the voice said.

"Yes," the king said decisively. "Tonight, I wish to be alone in the garden with the moon. Have a meal brought to me in the Clasping the Moon Pavilion and do not disturb me until morning."

"Yes, Your Majesty," the voice said. And Minli couldn't help but peek out. She saw rows and rows of finely dressed people kneeling with their heads on the ground in front of the king. Their rich silk clothing shimmered in the fading sunlight. One man, dressed in black, kneeled closer to the king, separate from the rest of the courtiers. Minli guessed he was Counselor Chu.

"Actually, bring me two meals," the king said, and glanced toward Minli. She caught his eye and quickly shrank back out of sight.

"Two meals, Your Majesty?" Counselor Chu asked with just the faintest question in his voice.

"Yes, two meals," the king said. "I shall honor the spirit

of the moon with her own meal, since she will be keeping me company. It is only fair."

"Yes, Your Majesty," the counselor said. Minli could only guess how puzzled he was, but he was well trained enough to keep it out of his voice.

"In an hour's time," the king said, "I shall be at the Clasping the Moon Pavilion. I want the food waiting for me and nothing else. I do not wish to be disturbed by anyone this evening."

"Yes, Your Majesty," the voice said again, and Minli could hear the shuffling and swishing of silk as the group rose and took leave of the king.

"They've gone," the king said in a low voice. "You can come out now."

Minli crawled out from behind the sculpture.

"Well, my little friend," he said to her, "now that you know who I am, come walk with me and tell me who you are."

CHAPTER
23

Minli and the king walked through the garden and she told him her name and where she was from and about her journey. Remembering the fish's warning, she carefully didn't mention Dragon waiting for her in the forest. As they walked, the patterned stone pathways gently massaged her feet and the sun seemed to disappear like a closing flower. When they finally approached the pavilion, night had fallen.

"So," the king said, "now you have come here to find the Guardian of the City."

"Yes," Minli said, and looked at him expectantly.

"And you think the guardian is me," the king said.

"Yes," Minli said. "Do you know what the borrowed line is? May I have it?"

"The borrowed line," the king repeated, and they stopped in front of the pavilion. The moon's reflection fastened onto the water's surface, and Minli saw why the pavilion was called Clasping the Moon. The image of the moon lay protected in the water like a glowing pearl, and the king stared at it deep in thought. "Come, let's eat and then we'll see what can be done about your borrowed line."

Minli entered the open-air pavilion. At the center, two stools and a small table of elaborately carved gingko wood waited for them. A large, finely woven bamboo basket as tall as Minli's waist stood next to the chairs. The king eagerly lifted off its lid and rich, warm aromas floated in the air, making Minli's stomach grumble.

The king took out the plates of delicate pink shrimp dumplings, savory noodles and pork, dragon's beard bean sprouts, emerald green chives, and a bowl of white jade tofu soup. A pot of tea and an assortment of cakes sat on the bottom layer of the basket, to finish off the dinner.

The king handed Minli a pair of intricate gold chopsticks that weighed heavily in her hands, and with his urging, Minli began to eat what was easily the most delicious meal she had ever had.

"I'm not sure what the borrowed line is that you are looking for," the king told Minli as he sipped his tea. They had finished eating the main meal and she was enjoying a turtle-shaped cake filled with sweet and soft red bean paste, a taste not known to her before. As she swallowed, its richness seemed to warm her from her throat to her stomach. "But I think I can guess."

With great effort, Minli stopped eating and looked at him. "You can?" she asked, and suddenly a hope filled her. "What do you think it is?"

"Do you know why this city is called the City of Bright Moonlight?" the king asked.

Minli shook her head.

"My great-great-grandfather changed the name of this city. It used to be called the City of the Far Remote. But after he came to power, he changed it to the City of Bright Moonlight," the king said. "Most people thought it was because he had a poetic heart. But it was more than that.

Have you heard the story of the magistrate that tried to outwit the Old Man of the Moon?"

Minli nodded. "He tried to kill his son's destined wife, but they ended up together anyway."

"Ah, you know the story." The king smiled. "That magistrate was my great-great-grandfather's father. And this city is the city that his son became king of through the marriage."

"So the story *is* real!" Minli said.

"Well, it is a story that has been passed through my family for generations," the king said. "But there's more to it than what most have heard."

THE UNKNOWN PART OF THE STORY OF THE OLD MAN OF THE MOON

After the Old Man of the Moon told the magistrate that his son would marry the daughter of a grocer, Magistrate Tiger flew into a rage. With both hands he grabbed the page and tore it from the book. But before he could rip the page in two, the Old Man's eyes stared into his and the light of the moon seemed to bind the magistrate still. As the silence hung in the air, Magistrate Tiger's anger turned to fear.

But, finally, the Old Man of the Moon nodded at him grimly. "Pages of the Book of Fortune do not tear easily, but that paper was being sent to you before I borrowed it," the Old Man said. "So perhaps it is only fitting that you finally receive it. Take it. The Book has bestowed some extra qualities to it, though they will be as useless to you as the original paper would have been."

And without another word, the Old Man of the Moon stood up and walked away up the mountain. The magistrate could do nothing but stare, clutching the ripped paper in dumbfounded silence.

"He tore a page out of the Book of Fortune?" Minli said.

"Yes," the king said, "but he, himself, was never able

to read it, so it remained useless to him just as the Old Man of the Moon had said it would be."

"Come," the king said as he walked out of the pavilion onto the bridge under the moon. As Minli followed, he reached inside the breast of his shirt, slowly took out a gold-threaded pouch, and said, "This is the ripped page. It has been passed down from generation to generation, studied by the kings of the City of Bright Moonlight. None of us has ever understood what the Old Man of the Moon meant when he said it was borrowed."

Minli watched, fascinated, as the king took from the gold pouch a delicate, folded piece of paper. Paler than even the white jade tofu she had eaten for dinner, the paper seemed to have a light of its own, dimming the gold threads of the pouch that held it.

"It was my great-great-grandfather," the king said, unfolding the paper, "who realized that the words on it can only be seen in the bright moonlight. He renamed the city the City of Bright Moonlight as a reminder for the kings that followed him."

Minli looked at the paper as if in a daze. In the moonlight, the page glowed. A single line of faint words, as if written with shadows, was scrawled upon the page in a language Minli had never seen.

"So, I think this paper, which the Old Man of the Moon said he borrowed," the king said, "this written line torn from the Book of Fortune is 'the borrowed line' you seek."

"Of course," Minli said, and excitement bubbled inside of her, "it must be!" But her excitement popped as she looked at the carefully preserved page and remembered how the king had had it on his person, carefully and preciously kept in the pouch around his neck. It seemed impossible that he would give her such a cherished treasure.

"It was only after much study that my great-great-grandfather was able to decipher the words," the king said. "And that is when he realized that the words changed according to the situation at the time. From then on, whenever a King of the City of Bright Moonlight has had a problem, he consults the paper."

"And it tells you what to do?" Minli asked.

"Yes." The king gave a wry smile. "Though not the way you think. Sometimes the line on the page is more mysterious than the problem."

And with that, the king looked down at the line. As he read, a startled expression came across his face.

"What does it say?" Minli asked.

"It says," the king said slowly, *"You only lose what you cling to."*

The king's words seemed to hang in the air. All was silent except for the soft rustling of the page in the gentle breeze. Minli, unable to speak, watched it flutter as if it were waving at her.

"So, it seems your request," the king said, "deserves consideration. The line tells me as much. Let me think."

Minli looked at the king, quiet but puzzled.

"For generations, my family has prized this paper; we have honored it for its spiritual power and authority. It has been passed on and studied and cherished and revered. It has been valued above gold or jade," the king said slowly. "But what is it really?"

Minli shook her head, unsure if she should respond.

"It is, actually," the king said, "simply proof of my ancestor's rudeness, his unprincipled anger and ruthless greed. Yet we've disregarded that — instead we guard and protect this written line so dearly that the rulers of the City of Bright Moonlight carry it at all times, not daring to let it out of their possession."

The moon seemed to tremble as ripples spread over its reflection caught in the water. The king continued, again, speaking more to himself than to Minli.

"We have clung to it, always afraid of losing it," the king said. "But if I choose to release it, there is no loss."

Minli felt her breath freeze in her chest. She knew the king's mind was in a delicate balance. If he refused to give her the line now, she knew she would never get it.

"And perhaps it was never meant for us to cling to. No matter whom the paper originally belonged to, this is a page from the Book of Fortune — a book that no one owns," the king said. "So, perhaps, it is time for the paper to return to the book."

A wind skimmed the water, and Minli could see her anxious face as pale and as white as the moon reflected in it.

"You only lose what you cling to," the king repeated to himself. He glanced again at the paper and then looked at Minli. A serene expression settled on his face and then he quietly smiled and said, "So, by choosing to give you the line, I do not lose it."

And, with those words, he placed the paper in Minli's trembling hands.

CHAPTER
24

Outside the city, Dragon waited. Even after Minli had disappeared, the dragon still watched from the trees. He had felt odd when she had passed the old stone lions and the door had closed behind her. He realized that he had never had a friend before, and what a nice feeling it was to have one.

And perhaps that was why the second night, when the sky darkened and the moon rose, Dragon crept out from the shadows of the trees and approached the closed, sleeping city. While he wouldn't admit it, Dragon thought just standing by the walled city might make him feel just a bit less lonely.

The silver moon cast a frosted glow upon the rough stone wall and guardian lion statues. Dragon stared at them as he approached the gate. Their stocky, heavily built bodies seemed to weigh down the stone platforms they sat upon; and the darkness of the night made their stiff, curly manes look like rows of carved blossoms. One lion held a round ball underneath his forearm; the other held down a lion cub that seemed to be grinning at him. In fact, all the lions seemed to be grinning at him as if he were a secret joke they were watching.

"Am I so funny?" Dragon asked them as he passed.

"YES!" burst out the small lion cub, wriggling free of his mother's paw. "You're very funny!"

As Dragon jumped back in surprise, the lion cub laughed out loud, obviously highly amused at the dragon's shock. But with his laugh, both adult lions shook themselves from their platforms.

"Xiao Mao!" the mother lion scolded. "Don't laugh at the lost dragon. Besides, you know the rules. No moving in the presence of others."

"But it's a dragon," the cub said, "not a people. He doesn't count for the rules, does he? Besides, he is funny! Big dragon trying to tiptoe like a mouse!"

"Xiao Mao," the deep, male voice of the other lion boomed in the air. The cub gave a halfhearted look of shame and was immediately quiet and still.

By this time, Dragon had found his voice.

"You're alive, then," he said.

"Of course we are," the male lion said, scrutinizing the dragon with interested eyes. "Everything's alive — the ground you're walking on, the bark of those trees. We were always alive, even before we were lions and were just raw stone. However, carving us did give us a bit more personality."

"You're a fairly young dragon, aren't you?" the female lion said kindly. "You seem only a hundred or a hundred and fifty years old. Don't worry, you'll learn soon enough."

"A hundred!" the lion cub said. "I'm much older than you. I'm eight hundred and sixty-eight!"

"And you still have not attained wisdom," the father lion told him. "Don't tease the young one."

"Well, what are you doing here?" the cub asked, not

unkindly. "Dragons don't usually come down to the earth much. Are you lost?"

Though unusual, the lions weren't unfriendly, so Dragon settled down and told them the whole story — being born, living in the forest, meeting Minli, and now their travels to find the borrowed line and the Old Man of the Moon. The lions didn't interrupt once, though the cub did snicker from time to time.

"You belonged to Magistrate Tiger?" the cub said when Dragon had finished. "That means you're the terrible dragon! You're the one that destroyed the king's father's palace. What a lot of trouble you caused!"

Dragon looked at the older lions questioningly.

"About one hundred years ago," the female lion said, "the king's father fled his home village. A dragon had destroyed his palace and his people had cast him out, saying he was bad luck. He came here, intending to make his home with his son and to live off his son's wealth and power as the King of the City of Bright Moonlight. There were bad times here for the city, as the king's father and the officials he brought with him were corrupt and greedy. We were very concerned."

"You?" the dragon asked. "Why would it concern you?"

"Why would it concern us? It is completely our concern!" the male lion said. "We are the Guardians of the City. It's our responsibility to watch and keep the city turning. To see it begin to crack alarmed us to no end." And the lion held out the round ball he held in his hand and showed Dragon an old, deep fracture that was slowly being filled with the dust of the earth.

"What did you do?" Dragon asked.

A STRING OF DESTINY

We were afraid the city would break. As the times became more turbulent with secret meetings and violent outbursts, we watched the crack in our world widen. It was only a matter of time, we thought, before it would tear into two.

One night, as we despaired, we saw a figure walking in the moonlight. Bent and old, he glowed like a lit lantern. When we saw he was carrying a large book and a small sack, we knew instantly it was the Old Man of the Moon and called him over.

"Please help us," we begged him, "we need to keep the city together."

The Old Man of the Moon looked at us, our out-stretched cracking globe, and our pleading faces. Without a word, he sat down before us and opened his book, leafing through the pages and stroking his beard.

After several minutes of consulting his book, he opened his sack and handed us a red thread.

"You are to hold this until it is needed," the Old Man told us, and then slapped his book shut and walked away, ignoring our words of thanks.

We knew the Old Man of the Moon had given us a string of destiny, one of the very strings he used to bind people together. It was a marvelous gift. While he left us no instructions, we guessed that we were to use it to tie around the city if it looked as if it were to split.

After that, night after night, we watched our sphere, ready to use the string at the first signs of breakage.

Unsure of its power or abilities, we dared not use it for anything but the direst of circumstances.

But the crack did not grow. Unexpectedly, the king renounced his father. He exiled him and his officials from the city and harmony returned. Slowly, the fracture has filled with the powder of earth and stone. And I have held the string, unused.

And as the male lion finished, he lifted his paw, to reveal a flattened line of red thread.

"The borrowed line!" Dragon said. "That's it! Minli said she needed to get the borrowed line from the Guardian of the City! You're the guardian and that's the borrowed line we need!"

"I suppose it is," the lion said, looking at the string. "So, perhaps I have been holding it all this time so I could give it to you."

And the lion dropped the string into the dragon's outstretched hand.

CHAPTER
25

Ma and Ba found the days without Minli long and difficult. In the morning, as soon as they woke up, they rushed
to Minli's bed to see if she was there. In the afternoon,
they hurried from the fields, hoping to find Minli waiting
at home. And at night, with a rice bowl and a set of chopsticks waiting for her at the table, they looked up at every
sound of footsteps.

But an empty bed and house always greeted them, and
the footsteps always belonged to a passing neighbor. While
Ma's anger had disappeared with the goldfish man, she

grew a little thinner and paler every day, and Ba's eyes no longer twinkled.

And one evening, in the middle of the night, Ba woke up alone in bed to a voice calling.

"Wake up, old man!" the fish said. "Wake up! Your wife needs you."

Ba quickly rose and looked for Ma, who was sitting by Minli's bed. In the stillness of the darkness, Ma shook with sobs.

"Oh, Wife," Ba said softly, sitting next to her.

Ma turned to him, her face shiny from wet tears. "What if Minli never returns?" Ma said. "What if we are always without her?"

Ba put his hand over his face, brushing away the tears that were forming in his eyes. "I don't know," he said.

"Neither do I," Ma said, and she buried her face in Minli's bed, crying in despair.

Ba stroked her hair as she wept, occasionally closing his eyes as he fought his own gloom. Finally, as Ma's crying slowed and calmed, Ba said, "Do you remember the story I told you about the paper of happiness? And the secret, which was one word written over and over again?"

The back of Ma's head nodded and Ba allowed himself a small smile.

"I have thought a long time about what that word could have been," Ba said. "Was it wisdom or honor? Love or truth? For a long time I liked to think that the word was kindness."

Ma's face remained hidden in Minli's bed, but her sobs had stopped and Ba knew she was listening.

"But now," Ba said, "I think, perhaps, the word was faith."

A faint, gray light seeped into the room, as if the moon was escaping from the clouds. Ma lifted her head and looked at Ba again. She wiped her eyes with her sleeve and gave him a small, sad smile.

"Perhaps," she said, "perhaps, you are right."

And she placed her hand, wet with tears, in his.

CHAPTER
26

The next morning, Minli woke up alone under a heavy, rich blanket. Even though she was on the floor of the garden pagoda, she had slept comfortably, and as she sat up she realized that was probably due to the silk pillows she had been lying on. The soft sunlight cast leaf shadows across her face and the wind made gentle ripples in the moss-colored lake in front of her. The Imperial Garden was just as beautiful in the day as it was by night.

On one side of her lay a small table with a small pot of tea, a bowl of rice porridge, and tea-stained eggs. "Breakfast," Minli thought to herself, but before she reached for it she saw that a yellow brocade traveling bag lay on the other side of her. Inside the bag, Minli found her humble blanket, rabbit rice bowl (with needle and bamboo piece), chopsticks, a generous supply of cakes, and her hollow gourd full of fresh water. On the very top lay the gold threaded pouch that held the ripped page of fortune. Minli took the pouch and held it with two hands.

Well, I have the borrowed line, Minli thought. *At least I hope it is.*

So after a quick breakfast, Minli quietly left the pavilion. Part of her was tempted to explore the mosaic walkways through the jewel-colored leaves, but she knew being discovered by one of the king's counselors would be disastrous. Also, she knew Dragon was patiently waiting outside the city. So, using the king's secret door, Minli carefully left the garden and walls of the Inner City.

And when she was out of the garden, Minli realized it

was very early morning. The Outer City was still sleeping; the stands were bare and the umbrellas were closed. Quickly, Minli scurried to the gate. With great effort she was able to get through — she had to use a metal pole she'd found on the ground to lift the lock and lever one of the doors open. Even then, she was only able to get it open a crack and had to squeeze.

As she fell through the gate, gasping for air, she was shocked to see Dragon lying in front of the stone lions, sleeping.

It took a couple of prods before Dragon woke, and his loud morning yawns almost put Minli in a panic, but they were able to get back to the hiding shelter of the forest before anyone saw them.

"What were you doing by the city?" Minli asked. "You were supposed to stay hidden!"

"I was getting the borrowed line," Dragon said.

"What do you mean?" Minli said. "I have the borrowed line."

And in a rush, the two of them told each other about their night adventures. Dragon stared at the ripped page from the book and Minli looked at the red cord in Dragon's hand.

"So which is the real borrowed line?" Dragon asked Minli.

"I guess that is another question we'll have to ask the Old Man of the Moon," Minli said.

CHAPTER
27

With both borrowed lines, Minli and the dragon continued their journey. Minli remade her compass with her rabbit rice bowl and followed the needle's pointed direction. As they traveled, the land became more barren, rocky, and steep. Without trees to tame it, the wind blew wildly, burning Minli's cheeks red with cold. The icy air shoved and pushed them, as if trying to keep them back.

Late in the afternoon, after traveling up stony ground, Dragon made a noise. "Look up ahead," he said.

Far ahead of them seemed to be a spot of bright yellow.

Against the gray landscape it seemed like a fallen piece of gold.

"Is it a forest? Trees with yellow leaves?" Minli asked, then she looked at the gray stone surrounding them. "But what trees could grow here?"

"I think there is a village," Dragon said, squinting his eyes. "If there is, we can get you some warmer clothes." Even though the cold hadn't bothered the dragon, he had noticed her shivering.

"We won't reach it before night," Minli said, "but I think there's a cave up ahead. Let's stay there for the night and tomorrow we'll try to reach the village or whatever it is."

The dragon agreed and they made camp in the cave. The king's supply of traveling cakes saved her and Dragon from hunger, but Minli wished for the thick silk blanket. Even in the shelter of the cave, away from the wind, the earth was stark and cold. Minli built a fire as quickly as she could and sighed as its warmth slowly heated the air.

But that night, Minli could not fall asleep. Even with the dragon snoring behind her, the fire crackling, and her blanket around her shoulders, her eyes did not close. Like the stone dust that the wind blew, thoughts kept circling in her head. She kept thinking about Ma and Ba and the orphan buffalo boy. With pangs of guilt, she thought about how Ma and Ba pushed her to go home early from the field, how her rice bowl was always the first filled, how every night when she went to sleep in her warm bed she knew they were there, and how worried they must have been that now she was not. The buffalo boy didn't have that. Instead he had a dirt floor, a pile of grass for his bed, a muddy buffalo, and a secretive friend. Yet he turned away her copper coin and laughed in the sun. Minli couldn't quite understand it and, somehow, felt ashamed.

But just as Minli shook her head with confusion, there was a sudden sound outside the cave. What was that? She cocked her head. There it was again, like a low grumble of thunder. Was it going to rain? Minli quietly got up and slipped out of the cave to see.

But when she got outside, she screamed! The noise had not been the grumble of thunder, it had been a growl of a TIGER! The giant tiger snarled and then jumped right at Minli!

CHAPTER
28

The wind screamed as Ma and Ba ate their dinner. The shutters of their house waved and slammed, shaking the house, and the light from their lantern wavered. They looked at each other and wordlessly went to the window.

"There is fear in the wind," the fish said, "great worry."

"Is it a storm?" Ma asked.

Ba looked at the fish. It stared at him with big eyes.

"I'm not sure," Ba said.

The tree branches bent in the wind violently, as if being shaken by the sky. The wind shrieked again, and the cold air gusted into the house. The water in the fishbowl rippled and the fish swayed in the bowl. Both Ma and Ba shivered.

"Do you think Minli is outside in this . . ." Ma faltered.

"I hope not," Ba said. The wind continued to slap the house and trees, the whole earth seemed to shudder at the screeching wind. Only the moon above was still.

Ba looked at Ma and saw her soundless lips move as she gazed at the moon. He knew what she was doing and did the same.

"Please," he implored the moon, silently, "please watch over Minli. Please keep her safe."

The moon continued to shine.

CHAPTER
29

Minli's scream seemed to freeze in the air. The tiger leapt at her, his scowling mouth glittering with pointed teeth, his blade-like claws rushing toward her. Minli knew there was no escape.

But! A flash of red violently knocked the attacking claw away. Minli gasped as Dragon roared, the tiger's claws ripping into his arm. With the brutal force of his other arm, the dragon threw the tiger back — forcing it to fly in the air.

"GO AWAY!" Dragon thundered, in a voice that even made Minli quake. She would never have imagined Dragon could speak that way.

The tiger glared like a spoiled child. Minli could now see it was not an ordinary tiger. It was bigger than a horse or buffalo and it was a dark, dusty green like the color of sand dirtied from ocean foam. Even in the dim light of the moon, Minli could see its eyes glower with malevolence.

"GO!" Dragon commanded again. Minli realized she had forgotten how big Dragon was. The tiger was large, but Dragon was bigger — though the viciousness of the tiger's expression made them seem evenly matched.

But the tiger gave another malicious snarl and turned away. Dragon stood his full height until even the tiger's moonlit shadow disappeared from view.

"Are you all right?" Dragon asked finally.

"That tiger . . . ," Minli said in a daze, "that tiger was going to kill me!"

"I know," Dragon said. "That tiger was truly evil. When you screamed, I could feel it."

And strangely, without knowing why, Minli burst into tears. The tiger's roars still echoed in her ears and she could still see his cruel claws and eyes. Now that he was gone, her terror flooded out of her.

"It is okay," the dragon said, gently putting his arm on her shoulders.

It was then Minli saw the four long gashes bleeding on Dragon's arm. The tiger's claws had been sharp and the slashes were deep. Minli shook herself and brushed her tears away. "You're hurt," Minli said, looking at the cuts, which were already starting to swell.

"It is all right," Dragon said. "Don't worry. Dragons heal quickly."

They walked back into the cave and Minli poured water on the wounds to clean them. She wrapped her blanket around Dragon's arm, but it continued to slowly bleed. As he lay down, Minli noticed Dragon's eyes fade and blur.

"I am starting to feel strange," Dragon said huskily. "Perhaps I will sleep."

"Okay," Minli said, "you sleep. Maybe when you wake up, you'll feel better."

But Minli felt as if she had swallowed a frozen rock. Something was wrong with Dragon. She knew it. Throughout the night, his breathing grew hoarser and his skin was damp. Every time she unwrapped the blanket, she grimaced — the ugly wounds had turned black, and evil-looking liquid was starting to seep. Minli shivered, and it was not from the cold.

He's getting weaker, Minli thought. *Something is very wrong. I have to do something. Dragon needs help. But I don't want to leave him. What am I going to do?*

By the time the first light of the sun crept into the cave, Dragon's breathing was rough; when Minli shook him, he did not wake up. Minli felt a surge of panic. *I don't know what to do,* she thought desperately. Her quick-thinking mind darted like a flustered butterfly. *I know,* she thought. *I'll go to that village. Maybe someone there will know what to do.*

Minli stood up and whispered into Dragon's ear, "I'm going to get help. I'll be back soon, I promise. Just hold on until then, okay?"

But Dragon did not respond and Minli felt tears start

to form in her eyes. Quickly, without even gathering her things, she turned and left.

It was mid-morning outside and Minli squinted in the sun. The wind still blew bitterly, but she didn't even notice. Instead, Minli began to run toward the patch of yellow in the distance.

CHAPTER
30

Minli's feet pounded against the rocky ground, fighting the uneven earth as she climbed upward. It was difficult. The wind-carved rocks and boulders seemed to grow from the ground like trees, confusing her way and disrupting her balance. Minli was so intent on her movement that she almost didn't notice a low growl. But she halted as soon as she heard it. The tiger!

She could see the tip of its green tail ahead over one of the large misshapen rocks. Quietly, she grabbed a sharp-looking stone from the ground and crept forward.

There it was, in a clearing of flat stone — the evil animal was pacing back and forth as if it were waiting. Minli tightened her grip on the stone.

Then she gasped. A plump little girl, dressed in brilliant red, was running toward the tiger! Before Minli could scream a warning, someone from behind her pulled her down and covered her mouth.

"Shhh!" the voice said, and Minli looked into the eyes of a small boy, who seemed to be the same age as the girl. Underneath a gray blanket he was using like a cape, she could see flashes of quilted red clothing that matched the girl's. His face was round and pink, as if it were more used to laughing than the serious frown it wore now. She nodded at his panicked gestures to keep quiet.

"Oh, Great Green Tiger!" The little girl threw herself on the ground in a trembling kowtow before the beast. "Powerful Spirit of the magistrate my worthless ancestors angered! My brother and I were sent to you as the sacrifice you demanded."

The tiger roared furiously and the girl cowered.

"I'm sorry," the girl said, her voice quivering. "My

brother and I were both sent to you, but on the way here, another monstrous beast attacked us! He took my brother and so there is only me."

The tiger made an outraged sound.

"Yes, another beast," the girl said. "This is what happened."

THE STORY THE GIRL
TOLD THE GREEN TIGER

Your message to the family caused an uproar. There was great wailing and crying as A-Gong, our grandfather, told us that you demanded two children every month to be sacrificed to you. It was payment for the insult our ancestors caused you, he said, and if we paid, you would leave the rest of the family in peace. It was a high price but we knew, with your immense power and strength, we could not disobey.

So my brother and I chose to be the first two children. As the family wept, my brother and I left our home to go to you. But as we made our way to meet you, an evil beast jumped from the rocks!

He looked like you — only not as strong or as mighty, of course. And he was dark, the color of a night shadow. He roared at us, but as we trembled to the ground I cried out, "Do not eat us, Beast! We belong to the Great Green Tiger!"

And the beast stopped his roar at my words. "Green Tiger?" he growled.

"Yes," I said. "We are sacrifices for the Great Green Tiger! We are not for you. If you attack us, you will make the mighty Green Tiger angry and he will destroy you!"

"Destroy me? Ha! Ha!" the beast laughed. "The Green Tiger is an old weakling!"

"No," my brother protested, "the Great Green Tiger is the most powerful beast of all! None can defy him!"

The beast laughed again, "A paper pig is more mighty than the Green Tiger! I will take you, but leave the other for him — pathetic dog that he is."

"And with that," the girl said, "he took my brother and dragged him to his cave."

The girl burst into sobs as Minli stole a glance at the boy. The boy looked a bit sheepish, but again put his finger to his lips for quiet. The tiger growled with impatience.

"As he disappeared he said . . . he said" — the girl swallowed nervously at the Green Tiger's furious face — "'Tell the Green Tiger that his son, the king, left you out of pity — pity for his poor, feeble father!'"

With those words, the Green Tiger roared with such rage that even the stones seemed to shudder. Minli quaked and the boy held her arm even tighter.

"I can show you his den where he dragged my brother," the girl quivered.

The tiger nodded at the girl with narrowed eyes seething with fury.

Shaking, the girl got up and began to lead the tiger away from the clearing. Minli, with the boy beckoning, silently followed.

CHAPTER
31

Minli and the boy followed from a distance, past sharp rocks and jutting boulders. The girl finally stopped in another clearing. It was only when Minli and the boy pressed up behind one of the rocks that she realized it was once a stone carving and the clearing was the ruin of an abandoned house, now mostly worn away by the wind.

"Here," the girl said. "The beast dragged my brother into that cave!" She pointed to a strange hole in the ground.

Minli scarcely recognized it as a large abandoned well. The rocks around the opening were rough and cracked;

and a ripped piece of red fabric lay torn on one of the sharp stones. Minli looked at the boy and saw his ripped pants. He smirked.

"The beast . . . your son" — the girl faltered — "is in there! He also said . . ."

The tiger growled at her to continue.

"He said that," and the girl swallowed in fear, "that you would be too much of a coward to confront him."

The tiger glowered ferociously, stalked to the edge of the well, and snarled into the blackness.

"He's in there," the girl said. "Do you see him?"

The deep well was full of shadows, but the dark water caught the reflection of the tiger's menacing eyes and sharp teeth. Full of wrath, the tiger growled at his own reflection, thinking it was a black beast. As the reflection growled back, the tiger gave a furious roar. The roar echoed back.

"That's him," the girl said. "He's mocking you!"

Outraged, the tiger clawed the stone ground and snarled again — even louder and angrier.

"How dare he!" the girl said. "He insults you! Your own son!"

The girl's words and his own echoing roars set the Green Tiger off into a frenzy. The air seemed to be charged with his uncontrollable fury — every hair on the tiger seemed to jut like sharp spikes, and his teeth and eyes glittered like the cutting edge of a knife.

He gave a deafening roar that bellowed, filling the sky with thunder. At its sound, the girl fell to the ground and Minli and the boy covered their ears. The tiger bared his teeth and claws for an attack. And when the roar echoed back, it overwhelmed him with wild rage. Finally, the Green Tiger gave one last roar and . . . leapt into the well!

The girl, boy, and Minli stood frozen as the air filled with roars and the sound of splashing water. Then, suddenly, the wind carried one last howl into the sky; there was silence. Minli stared in disbelief. The Green Tiger was gone!

CHAPTER
32

"We did it! We did it!" The boy and girl laughed as they ran to each other and hugged. They both were younger than Minli; she realized that they were twins — their round faces, dancing eyes, and pink cheeks were exactly the same. The gray blanket that the boy had used to help hide himself was thrown on the ground, and with their dimpled faces swollen with smiles and their matching, bright red clothing, they looked like two rolling berries. Minli couldn't help but smile.

And as they laughed and congratulated each other, another voice called in the distance.

"A-Fu! Da-Fu!" the voice cried. "Where are you?"

The children looked at each other. "A-Gong!" the girl said, and then together they called, "Here! We're over here!"

A tall, gray-haired man burst into the clearing; a bag was strapped onto his back and in one hand he held a sword and in the other a spear. As soon as he saw the children, both weapons clattered to the ground and they ran into his arms.

"A-Fu! Da-Fu!" he cried. "We were so worried!"

"We did it, A-Gong!" the boy said. "We did it! We destroyed the tiger just like we said we would!"

"Yes," the girl said. "Our plan worked! We tricked him into the well, just like we said we would!"

"You were not supposed to do that," the man said, holding them tightly. "We told you it was too dangerous!"

"That's why we sneaked away," the girl said. "We knew it would work . . . we used his anger against him just like you said we should! You said he was even angrier at his son and his anger would blind him . . . and it did!"

"I didn't say you should do anything," the man said, kneeling with his hands on both their shoulders. "You were not supposed to go after the Green Tiger yourselves."

"You're not angry, right?" the boy said. "Now, no one will have to be scared anymore. We can let the animals out of the house and go outdoors again!"

"Oh, Da-Fu!" the grandfather said, hugging them again even closer. "A-Fu! As long as you both are safe — that is all that matters."

Then the gray-haired man saw Minli watching them.

"Ah, who is this?" he said, beckoning Minli closer.

Before either child could say a word, Minli rushed up with a hurried bow.

"Please," she said, "my friend, the Green Tiger injured him and he's hurt and . . ."

The grandfather quickly pushed the children off of him and stood up. "Hurt by the Green Tiger!" he said. "Take me to your friend quickly. It is lucky I brought the medicine bag with me. Da-Fu, get your blanket and give it to this girl. She is cold."

The boy ran for his blanket, stopping to pick up the torn fabric from his pants, and brought it to her. Minli wrapped the gray blanket around her. She was grateful for its warmth but even more grateful that the man wanted to help immediately. "How long ago was your friend injured?" the man asked as he urged her to lead the way. After Minli told him, he shook his head. "We must hurry, then," he said. "The Green Tiger is no ordinary beast. His teeth and claws are poison. Without the medicine I have, he will die before seeing the sunset."

Minli swallowed hard and quickened her pace. The wind seemed to scream a warning, and even under the layer of Da-Fu's blanket, she felt cold. Would they be too late? Would they be able to save Dragon?

CHAPTER
33

"He's in here!" Minli called to A-Fu, Da-Fu, and their grandfather, pointing to the cave opening. Even before reaching the entrance, A-Gong was already holding the medicine bottle in his hand.

As they rushed inside, Minli was relieved to hear Dragon's rasping breath. He was still alive! But as the children and their grandfather saw him lying in the dim light, they stopped, shocked still.

"Your friend . . . your friend . . . ," the boy said in awe, ". . . is a dragon?"

The old man recovered from his surprise. "It matters not," he said to them. "Quickly, where is his wound?"

Minli carefully unwound her blanket from Dragon's arm and winced. The gashes seemed to have burned into him like evil coals; the blackness had spread and his arm looked like a burnt tree.

Swiftly, the man pushed Minli aside and began to pour the liquid from the medicine jar over Dragon's black arm. The tonic was a clear yellow-green, with a gentle aroma of fresh flowers and grass, reminding Minli of a spring morning. As it washed over Dragon's diseased arm, his tightly closed eyes relaxed and the grimace on his face smoothed — as if a deep pain was relieved. The medicine melted the dark poison; the blackness seemed to be rinsing away and Dragon's breathing became easier and even.

Minli sighed. She hadn't realized until then that she had been holding her breath. She knew, even before the man smiled, that Dragon was going to be okay.

"Da-A-Fu," the old man said, and Minli realized that he was calling both his grandchildren with a single name. "Go home and tell the family what has happened and where I am or they will worry. I need to stay with the dragon. Tell Amah and all the women to make more medicine and when it is ready, bring it to me. This dragon will need to drink it when he awakens."

"Thank you," Minli said softly.

The man turned and looked at her wind-burned face, tangled hair, and eyes shadowed with weariness. "He is going to be fine," the grandfather said to her kindly, and then turned back to the children. "Da-A-Fu — bring this girl home and tell Amah to take care of her. She has not slept in a warm bed for a long time."

"I want to stay with Dragon," Minli protested. "I want to help him."

"I will stay with him," the old man said to her. "Don't worry, he will be fine. You have already helped him."

Minli opened her mouth to argue, but a yawn formed instead. She realized the man was right and nodded her head. The boy took one of Minli's hands and the girl took the other and they led her out of the cave.

CHAPTER

34

"Which one of you is A-Fu and which one is Da-Fu?" Minli asked the twins. "My name's Minli."

The children laughed; their giggles were like bells playing in unison. "I'm A-Fu," the girl said, "he's Da-Fu. But you can just call us Da-A-Fu, because we are always together. Everyone does."

Minli smiled. The exhaustion from the long night of worry had made her feel heavy and clumsy, but the children's happiness seemed to carry her. Their every word seemed to be mixed with merriness; their laughter pushed her toward the cheerful yellow patch in the distance.

And as they approached the spot, Minli realized that the yellow was flowers — in front of them was land full of blooming trees. The trees were heavy with bright blossoms and as the wind blew through the branches, golden flowers showered down like rain.

As they reached the trees and breathed in the spicy scent of the flowers, Minli gasped. "It's beautiful," she said. The children laughed again, and the brilliant red of their clothes and the golden yellow flowers of the trees seemed to make Minli's eyes dazzle with color.

But their brilliance was a contrast to the stone rooftops of a village below. The homes looked as though they had to be hewed from the cold, harsh rock of the mountain; and Minli saw that the flowering trees were the only things that grew easily from the unforgiving rough soil. The boy saw Minli's gaze.

"That's our home," he told her, "the Village of the Moon Rain."

"Village of the Moon Rain?" Minli asked. "That's a

strange name. Why isn't your village named after the flowering trees?"

"It is," Da-Fu said.

THE STORY OF THE VILLAGE OF THE MOON RAIN

Over a hundred years ago, when our ancestors were first brought here, the land of the village was barren and gray. Everything was dull and colorless, the wind cold and bitter. Still, our ancestors worked hard. They built houses out of mountain stone, sewed warm, wadded-cotton jackets, and planted seeds in the hard dirt.

But, despite their efforts, the land refused to bear a single plant or flower. However, even though it looked hopeless, our ancestors continued to work.

Then one night, when the moon was big and round, the air filled with a strange fluttering sound. Our ancestors thought that a great storm was coming and rushed inside.

And a great storm *was* coming. With a crash, raindrops seemed to fall from the sky.

But what strange rain it was! Round and smooth, in the glowing light the raindrops looked like silver pearls! And when they touched the ground, they disappeared.

"It's raining pearls!" our ancestors said to each other. "Jewels from the moon!" And they rushed out with baskets and bags, catching what they could from this strange storm. Magically, when the raindrops were caught, they didn't disappear; and soon their baskets and bags were full.

But in the morning, our ancestors saw that the drops were not pearls or jewels. In the sunlight, they saw that they were really seeds. But no one knew what kind of seeds they were. Curious, they planted them in the hard earth.

And when the moon rose again that night, the strange rain fell again as well. This time our ancestors were not fooled and just watched the drops disappear

into the ground. But in the morning, the planted seeds were sprouting as if watered by a magic brew.

So night after night the seed rain fell from the sky. And as daylight broke over the land, the seedlings grew higher. Soon they grew into beautiful silver trees with golden flowers. They were so beautiful, our ancestors planted more and more seeds and soon the whole village was blooming with hundreds and hundreds of flowering trees.

And since then our home has been called the Village of the Moon Rain. We plant new seeds every day, and every night, the moon rain falls and every morning a new seedling sprouts. Maybe in another hundred years all this stony land will be covered with trees and the mountain will be as golden as the Moon.

"So these seeds rain from the sky every night?" Minli asked.

"Well, every night there is a moon," the girl said. "That is why we call it Moon Rain."

"And you don't know why?" Minli asked. Even though she was tired, she could not help being curious.

Both children shook their heads and before Minli could ask more questions the boy pointed. Minli followed his hand and saw crimson gate doors painted with a cheerful greeting.

"We're here!" he cried. "Come on, we're home!"

CHAPTER
35

After the great storm, Ma and Ba worried that vast damage had been done to the village. And when the sun shone in the morning, the village looked as if it were in ruins. Large tree branches had fallen and a clutter of leaves and roof tiles and dust and dirt littered the ground. Yet, when the villagers began to clean, they saw the storm had not harmed them as much as they had feared.

"At least no homes were destroyed," the villagers said to each other, "and we know everyone is safe."

Well, everyone except for Minli, they added silently.

Ma and Ba said nothing when their neighbors paused awkwardly. They helped pick up the broken branches, swept broken bits of pottery and tiles from the street, and nailed shutters. At night, they quietly sat together at the table with the goldfish. Though Ma had heard nothing, Ba remembered the fish's words about the fear in the wind. It filled him with worry and he waited for the fish to speak again. However, it remained oddly silent.

Finally, when Ma was busy helping a neighbor, Ba tried to question the fish.

"During the storm you said there was fear in the wind," Ba said to the fish. "Whose fear was it? Was it Minli's? Was she afraid of something?"

The fish stared at Ba with its round eyes and made no sound.

"Please tell me," Ba said, his hands around the bowl.

The fish swam noiselessly in the water.

Ba was puzzled. Had the fish stopped speaking? Or was he now unable to understand? Or perhaps the fish had never spoken and it all had been his imagination?

Ba placed his ear close to the water. Was that faint bubbling a whisper? He strained closer, his ear beginning to dip into the water . . .

"What are you doing?" Ma asked as she came into the room.

Ba jerked his head up, his ear dripping with water.

"Uh, nothing," he said sheepishly.

"Were you cleaning your ear in the fishbowl?" Ma said, slightly appalled.

"Not exactly," Ba said awkwardly.

A cross look streaked across Ma's face, but as she looked at Ba, rubbing his ear shamefacedly, she did something she hadn't done in years. She laughed.

"You look so silly! If Minli were here now," Ma said, "she would laugh at you."

"Yes, she would," Ba said, and he too began to laugh. "She would laugh until she cried."

Their laughter intertwined but when they looked at each other, they could see the tears forming were not from joy.

CHAPTER
36

Minli was so tired that she could barely remember what happened when they entered the village. She hardly remembered the clamor of people gathering around them and the loud cheers as Da-A-Fu told about the destruction of the Green Tiger. And she vaguely remembered the big, soft hug of an elderly woman who pushed her inside a welcoming house. But she did remember the cozy, lovely feeling of falling into a bed, like holding a warm steamed bun on an icy day. And then Minli closed her eyes and slept.

When she woke up, three round faces peered above her like plump peaches. They were Da-Fu, A-Fu, and Amah, their grandmother. Each of the children, dressed in their red wadded-cotton outfits (the rip in Da-Fu's pants was now patched), had little moveable stoves with them. With the heaters and all of them crowded in the room, Minli felt as if she were in a warm oven of kindness. She smiled.

"Good morning!" Amah said.

The children giggled. "Good night!" Da-Fu said. "You slept the whole day! Pretty soon it'll be time to go to bed again!"

"Now Da-A-Fu, don't tease the girl," Amah said. "Obviously, she was very tired. Here, Minli, drink this."

Amah poured some tea from a pot and handed Minli a cup. Minli sipped it gratefully. The steaming liquid slipped down her throat smoothly and seemed to fill every part of her with a fresh energy. She took another sip of tea and breathed in the tangy fragrance, which smelled familiar.

"This is nice tea," Minli said. "Thank you."

"It's not tea!" A-Fu said. "It's the medicine that cures the tiger's poison."

"It is tea as well," Amah said. "It is good whether you have been touched by the Green Tiger or not."

Minli stopped drinking. "Is there enough of this for the dragon?" Minli asked, remembering how A-Gong had asked them to bring more medicine. "Maybe we should take this to him."

Da-A-Fu laughed again. "Don't worry," they said, "we have a lot of it! It's made from the leaves of the flowering trees."

"And Da-A-Fu already brought a large pot to your dragon friend," Amah said, her wrinkled face looking kindly at Minli.

"Yes," A-Fu said. "Your dragon is doing fine. He and A-Gong were talking to each other when I brought the pot, and he even said thank you for saving him from the Green Tiger's poison."

Minli sat back, relieved and cheered by their words. "What was the Green Tiger? Da-A-Fu said something about a magistrate?" she asked. "And how did you know this tea cured the tiger's poison?"

"We found that out by accident," Amah said.

THE STORY OF
THE GREEN
TIGER AND THE TEA

When the Green Tiger discovered us four moons ago, we quickly learned he was not an ordinary tiger. It was not his color or his size, it was the anger he had for us. First, he attacked our livestock — the sheep, the pigs, the chickens — but not to eat, just to kill. He taunted us with his evil, leaving the dying animals in a row outside our door. Whatever animals he did not kill outright, died within an hour or so from the vile poison of the tiger's touch.

We knew it was just a matter of time before he caught one of us. We kept the children and whatever animals we had left inside. A-Gong, my husband, studied furiously, trying to find out more about this powerful monster who tormented us.

We were running out of food when A-Gong finally

discovered what the Green Tiger was. When A-Gong was a young man, he had made a journey to the city south of here and bought an old book of history. That book, with our ancestors' ancient texts, was how A-Gong discovered that the Green Tiger was the spirit of the magistrate our ancestors had tried to give the secret of happiness to, but had angered instead. During his life, the magistrate had filled his spirit with so much rage that when his body left, his spirit could not rest and instead turned into the Green Tiger. A-Gong learned that the Green Tiger searched for all those he felt had wronged him — the tiger would punish us for his imagined offense and then, when he felt the punishment was complete, destroy us; afterward he would find others who had wronged him and punish and destroy them as well. Who knows how many people he hurt before he came to us; perhaps we were lucky he only found us four moons ago.

In desperation, the men decided to form a hunting party to try to kill the tiger. But the Green Tiger was too powerful for us. Our swords and staffs were shattered by him. The hunting party returned, half of the men carried by the other half and almost all injured. The women and children, we tried to nurse the injured but they kept getting sicker and sicker from the tiger's poison and I began to despair.

Though it had not worked on any of the animals in the past, I thought perhaps hot water could wash away the poison from the wounds. So even though it was dangerous, I left the house to get water from the well. Just as I returned I saw the tiger!

He was standing in front of our gate, doing something peculiar. He seemed to be arranging things. I kept a far distance, behind the trunk of a flowering tree. He soon finished and left, not noticing me.

As soon as he left I carefully rushed to the gate. The tiger had left a strange array of objects. There was a piece of a broken vase with a moon on it, a mangled child's jacket, and two deep claw marks scratched into the stone. I knew it was a message, but what did it say? The only person who would know would be A-Gong. But he was sick and dying from the tiger's poison. My eyes filled with tears as I rushed inside.

It was hard for me to keep from crying and I was blinded by my own tears. So, it was only when the fragrance filled the air that I realized that the water I was boiling had leaves from the flowering trees in it. They must have fallen in while I was hiding from the Green Tiger. It was too dangerous to go and get more water — everyone was horrified that I had gone at all — so I used the hot leaf water to clean A-Gong's wound.

And like magic, the poison began to melt away. I couldn't believe it. I gave A-Gong some leaf water tea to drink, and immediately his hoarse breathing was soothed and his face relaxed. Quickly, we used the tea on all the men and by the time the last injured man was given the tea, A-Gong was sitting up in his bed with Da-A-Fu at his side.

"I was a fool," he said to us, "I should have known we could not fight the Green Tiger with more anger. We just add to his power that way. His anger is his strength, but it can also be his weakness. His anger can blind him, and that is when he is vulnerable. Maybe if I can find who angered the magistrate the most, I can . . ."

"You are definitely recovering." I had to smile. "Already you are making plans. But why don't you rest for now?"

"No." A-Gong waved away my concerns. "I must learn more, immediately, before the Green Tiger does more damage."

I knew then that A-Gong needed to see the Green Tiger's message right away. Da-A-Fu and I wrapped him in blankets and supported him as he hobbled to the gate. A-Gong looked grave as he examined the objects. Just as I thought, he knew right away what it meant.

"What is the Green Tiger saying?" A-Fu asked.

"It says if we give him two children every month, he will leave us in peace," A-Gong said. "This is the start of his punishment for us — the way we are to pay penance for our ancestors."

"How does it say that?" Da-Fu asked.

"Two claw marks next to a child's clothes means he wants two children, and the vase is a symbol of peace, the moon on it means every month. So he offers us a month of peace for two children," A-Gong said.

"It matters not, we will not sacrifice even a baby pig to him."

"But A-Fu and I had other ideas," Da-Fu said, interrupting. "After A-Gong found out that the person who angered the Green Tiger the most was his own son — he was a king and he had banished the Magistrate Tiger from the kingdom — we made a plan!"

"Yes," A-Fu said proudly, "we decided we would trick the Green Tiger into getting so angry that he would destroy himself in the well. And our plan worked!"

"It was also a plan that we did not approve of or agree to," Amah said, shaking her head at them, even though she could not help smiling affectionately. "But now young Minli, you have heard our story but we have not heard yours. We know your name and that you are friends with a dragon and we can guess you are far from home. Why don't you tell us the rest?"

So Minli told them about Ma and Ba, their struggles in the muddy fields, the goldfish man and the goldfish. She told them about meeting the dragon that could not fly and the monkeys and the buffalo boy. She told them about the King of the City of Bright Moonlight and the borrowed lines. She told them about her whole journey.

And as she spoke, Da-A-Fu and their grandmother laughed and gasped and stared in wonder. Sometimes Amah shook her head, sometimes Da-A-Fu would look at each other in disbelief. But they did not interrupt once.

"So all of this is to get to Never-Ending Mountain," Da-Fu said, finally. "We know where that is."

"You do?" Minli exclaimed, sitting up in excitement. "Really?"

"Yes, Never-Ending Mountain is nearby," A-Fu said. "About a day's journey."

Minli looked at them in shock and no words could come out of her mouth. A day's journey! After all their days of traveling, Minli couldn't believe they were so close.

"As soon as your dragon friend is well," Amah said, "Da-A-Fu will take you there. And then you can return to your parents."

Minli smiled gratefully, but as she looked at their comfortable, round, pink faces — how both A-Fu and Da-Fu leaned against their grandmother with devotion and how she rested her hands on their heads with tenderness — Minli suddenly thought of Ma and Ba. A wave of longing washed through her and a dryness caught in her throat that the tea could not moisten.

CHAPTER
37

The next morning, Da-A-Fu shook Minli awake.

"Wake up, sleepy!" Da-Fu said, pulling her up. "Come on! We want to show you something."

"Yes," A-Fu said, "hurry!"

Minli followed them out of the house and through the streets. It was almost as if there were a parade, for all the family were coming out of their houses and following. Minli hadn't realized Da-A-Fu's family was so large. There were aunts, uncles, cousins — the home behind the red gate doors was really a village of relatives. As

Minli ran around through the open doors, she stopped and grinned. Because there, waiting out on the stone ground, was Dragon!

He was strong and smiling, sitting straight and alert. There was no daze in his eyes and no foul blackness on his body — in fact, except for four pale raised scars on his arm, he looked exactly as he did before they met the Green Tiger. "You're okay!" Minli said as she hugged him.

"Of course," Dragon said to her, grinning with happiness. "I told you that dragons heal quickly."

"Yes, they do," A-Gong said from beside her. "After the poison left him, his wounds healed almost immediately."

Minli was so happy to see the dragon that she didn't notice that most of Da-A-Fu's family were surrounding them in awe.

"A dragon," she heard one small boy whisper, "a real one."

"We told you so," Da-A-Fu murmured to their cousins. "See!"

"Unfortunately, friend dragon," A-Gong said loudly so that all could hear, "you are too large for us to show you proper hospitality inside our home."

"That's okay. We should leave soon, anyway," Minli said, and turned to Da-A-Fu, "if you will still show us the way to Never-Ending Mountain?"

"Of course." They grinned and Amah said, "Yes, you should leave as soon as you can. The sooner you leave, the sooner you can return to your parents. That would be for the best."

A-Gong nodded when he heard Amah's words. "Breakfast, then," he said, "and then we will see our new friends off."

So even though the rocky land was cold and windy, the family brought their breakfasts of warm rice porridge out to eat. No one wanted to miss a moment of looking at a real dragon.

Amah led a large iron pot, rolled in on a rough wood platform by two of Da-A-Fu's uncles, in front of the dragon. The pot was steaming and full, and Minli recognized it as the medicine tea. An aunt carried cups of the tea on two trays balanced on her shoulders with a stick for anyone to take. Minli carefully reached for a cup; the fragrant aroma was too tempting to let pass.

"We should not call this drink medicine," an uncle said.

"It is too delicious and now that there is no more Green Tiger, there is nothing for it to cure."

"Maybe we should call it Well Tea," A-Fu laughed, "since the Green Tiger is down in the well."

"No," A-Gong said, "we want to remember our friends, not our enemies."

"Then we should call it Dragon Well Tea," Da-Fu said, "because it made the dragon well!"

The family all cheered at that, and there was a look of softness in Dragon's eyes that Minli had never seen before. He was unused to kindness, she realized. He had spent most of his years alone and trapped by his flightless body.

Too soon, breakfast was over and Minli was packing her possessions into the yellow silk bag the king had given her while Amah tied supplies onto the backs of A-Fu and Da-Fu. "Just in case," she said, slipping in their simple food of rice wrapped up in leaves and salted boiled eggs. "Bring Minli to Never-Ending Mountain and then come right home."

A-Gong put his hands on Minli's shoulders and said,

"You're a brave girl, Minli, quick and clever. But you have been away from home too long. Go as quickly as you can."

Amah wrapped her warm arms around Minli, then brought out a warm jacket. "For you," she said. "We made it while you were sleeping. Your dress is too thin for the mountain. "

The jacket was multicolored, made of large patches sewn together — some dark blue, some deep purple, a few bright red. Minli smiled thankfully; already the cold wind was chilling her but she was hesitant to ask these people for anything since they had already given her so much. As she put it on, she marveled at its warmth. The fabric looked like plain cotton, but she felt as warm as if she had put on a thick fur.

"Let's go then!" Da-A-Fu said, and the boy swung up his arm in excitement. It was only then that Minli noticed a large gash missing from his sleeve. She looked at the sleeve of her new coat and the bright red patch that made it and she gasped.

"Goodbye!" Da-A-Fu's family waved. As they waved, Minli saw each of them had missing material in their sleeves. Her goodbyes froze in her throat as she realized her warm coat was made of pieces cut from the family's own clothing.

"Come on," A-Fu said, her white hand slipping from her notched sleeve to pull at Minli. "Hurry up!"

"Yes," Dragon said, "we should go so the twins can return to their village as soon as possible."

Minli nodded — and as she waved a grateful goodbye to the village, a sea of ruined sleeves fluttered back at her.

CHAPTER
38

As Minli and Dragon followed Da-A-Fu up the harsh landscape, the wind blew wildly. But traveling was not difficult. Dragon carried them over any large cracks or openings; Minli had forgotten how enjoyable it was to travel with him. And Da-A-Fu, laughing with pure delight as they rode Dragon, looked like two ripe hawthorn berries. Their merriment and the brilliant red color of their clothes and of Dragon himself seemed to warm the cold landscape. It was only when Minli's hands poked out of her sleeves into the icy air that she realized how cold it really was.

"It's not much farther," A-Fu said to them after they had walked some distance. "We should be able to see Never-Ending Mountain soon."

"You've never seen the Old Man of the Moon though?" Minli asked. "Has anyone?"

Da-A-Fu shook their heads. "No one has ever seen him," Da-Fu said. "No one in the history of our family or village."

"Though we do know he is the one who moved our ancestors here," A-Fu said.

"The Old Man of the Moon brought your ancestors here?" Minli asked. "How?"

THE STORY OF DA-A-FU'S ANCESTORS

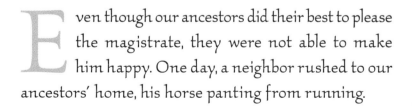

Even though our ancestors did their best to please the magistrate, they were not able to make him happy. One day, a neighbor rushed to our ancestors' home, his horse panting from running.

"I have just returned from the city," the neighbor gasped. "I rushed all the way here to warn you. The magistrate is convinced the answer you sent him was a trick and you are keeping the real secret from him. He is coming here to punish you. He plans to destroy your home and family! Run away while you can! There is not much time — his soldiers will be here tomorrow!"

Our ancestors cried with fear. The large family — the many sons and daughters, aunts and uncles, and children and grandchildren — could not help being scared. But Ye Ye, the great-grandfather and head of the family, raised his hand for attention.

"It looks as if misfortune is coming," he said, "and there is nothing we can do. We will not run. The soldiers would easily find us and the magistrate would be even more brutal. And I do not want to spend our last moments together in panicked flight."

Ye Ye looked at the bright blue sky and sun shining on the mountain beyond their home. It was hard to imagine the coming trouble. "Little ones," he said to the children, "go fetch your favorite kites." Then Ye Ye turned to the adults. "Sons and daughters," he said, "prepare the finest picnic you can, with enough food and tea for all. We will not waste this time we have together. We will spend it as we always have, in happiness."

The family nodded at Ye Ye's wise words. Quickly, they rushed to do as he asked. They brewed large pots of their best chrysanthemum tea and filled special baskets with golden cakes and custard tarts, boiled chickens, crispy pork, fluffy steamed buns, and tea-stained eggs. And their brilliant kites, in the shapes of bugs and butterflies, were dragged out of storage and into the sun.

Ye Ye smiled at his family as they finished their tasks. He carried his favorite books of poetry, stories, and songs in a bag. "Come," he said, "let us climb the mountain."

So together, with the tree leaves waving farewell, the family made their way up the mountain. They climbed high, so the kites could fly without the trees getting in the way. When there was nothing between them and the sky, they stopped.

And they had a delightful time. The children laughed as their kites soared in the wind. The women smiled as they sipped the tea and the men happily ate the delicious treats. Ye Ye recited poetry that made the women sigh, told stories that made the men gasp, and sang songs that made all the children join in.

But all too soon, the day was ending. The moon was already rising in the sky when the children were told to wind the strings of their kites.

"Why bring the kites down?" an older boy asked. "This will be the last time we will be able to play with them."

"Yes," a girl said. "Let them fly for as long as they can."

So instead of bringing the kites in, they cut the strings. As the kites were freed, a strong gust of wind burst from the sky. One by one, the butterflies and dragons disappeared as if flying home to the moon. As the kites vanished from sight, there was a sad sigh. No one spoke, but they all wished for an escape from tomorrow's tragedy.

Quietly, the family packed their belongings and began to climb down the mountain. They walked a long time, so long that the moon rose overhead and they began to shiver with cold.

"Are we lost?" a child asked. "This does not look like the way home."

"That's impossible," his mother told him. "How can we be lost? There is no other direction than down."

"But the boy is right," Ye Ye said. "Look at the rock before us. We have climbed this mountain many times yet I have never seen this rock or any rock of this type before."

"And there are no trees," a young girl said. "Always there were trees below us, and now there is just more rock."

"It's colder too," another said. "It is much too cold for an early autumn night."

"What has happened?" a woman asked.

"I think," Ye Ye said slowly, "we are no longer on our mountain. Somehow we are on a different one."

"How is that possible?" a man asked. "And why?"

Before Ye Ye could open his mouth to reply, one of the children shouted.

"Home!" she cried. "Our home is right there!"

And it was their home — the dark red gate doors were wide open, allowing them to see light shining from the windows of their houses. Their chickens squawked a greeting, and their dogs jumped through the gate with cheerful barks.

Our ancestors couldn't believe it. Dirty pots and pans that they had left in the morning were still in the washbasin, mixed-up shoes and hanging laundry were exactly where they were before. Even the book that Ye Ye had left was open on the same page. Ye Ye walked from room to room and house to house, with the family following like a parade. Finally, he found a slip of bright silk stuck in the hinges of the gate doors. He turned around to look at the family crowding about him.

"It is a miracle," he said to them. "We have been moved here, beyond the magistrate's reach. We are saved!"

The family cheered, but could not help asking, "How? Who did this?"

Ye Ye looked at the empty land around him and the dark blue sky with the moon above and then at the thin strip of silk in his hand. "This silk is from one of the children's kites. The kites brought our wishes up to the Old Man of the Moon and he must have decided that our destinies lay here," Ye Ye said, and he motioned upward. "For there is only one other here with us tonight. It is only us and the moon."

"And your family has been here ever since?" Dragon asked.

Both children nodded. "For over a hundred years, our family has lived on the mountain, and we keep growing. Sometimes we travel down the mountain, sometimes people come to us; anyone who visits is welcome to call our place home."

"So . . . ," Minli began, but her words died away as Da-Fu pointed toward the horizon. Minli and Dragon followed his hand and finally saw what could only be Never-Ending Mountain, home of the Old Man of the Moon.

CHAPTER
39

Never-Ending Mountain was enormous, so large that it made Fruitless Mountain seem like a loose pebble. Minli could not see the tip or the bottom of it, as it seemed to grow out of a gorge so deep that the base must have been at the foundation of the earth. Minli felt as if she were on the edge of the world as she stared across the great gulf separating them from the Never-Ending Mountain. It stood before them like a piece of raw green stone towering forever into the sky and disappearing into silver mist.

"There it is," Da-Fu said, "Never-Ending Mountain!"

"I bet the Old Man of the Moon does live up there," A-Fu said. "The top of this mountain must reach the moon."

"How do we get up there?" Minli asked. She was starting to feel dizzy from staring upward so long.

The dragon looked chagrined. "If I could fly," he said, "I'd be able to get us up there to see the Old Man of the Moon."

"If you could fly," A-Fu laughed, "you would not need to see him!"

"But," Minli said, "it looks like flying is the only way up to see the Old Man of the Moon."

"There's probably another way," A-Fu said.

"Yes," Da-Fu said, "you probably just have to let the Old Man of the Moon know you'd like to come up."

"How do we that?" Dragon asked. "Send a message?"

Minli looked up at the sky as Dragon and Da-A-Fu continued to talk. *Send a message, send a message.* Dragon's words echoed in Minli's ears and she felt as if she were searching for a match to light a lantern. The wind gusted at her, as if it were trying to tell her something. She watched

A-Fu's braid fly in the air; as she pulled it down, the cut pieces of her sleeve flapped like the tail of a kite . . .

"I know!" Minli said excitedly. "We'll do it like your ancestors did!" She quickly kneeled on the ground and reached in her traveling bag for the two borrowed lines. Dragon and the children looked at her curiously as she waved the sheet of paper and the string before them.

"We can fly a kite up to the Old Man of the Moon," Minli exclaimed. "I'll make a kite of the two borrowed lines, that's bound to get his attention."

Da-A-Fu and the dragon grinned and together they made the borrowed lines into a kite. They fastened the page from the Book of Fortune onto Minli's chopsticks and attached an end of the red cord to the kite. But as they tried to trim the thread — A-Fu thought it would look neater if the end didn't dangle — they discovered that the borrowed line could not be cut.

"It is a string of destiny," Dragon said as he tried again without success to cut the thread with his claw. Each of them, in succession, had tried to break it — Da-Fu even tried to snap it with his teeth. "It is reasonable to think it is unbreakable."

"Well, we don't need to trim the string to make the kite," Minli said. "But we can't cut the kite free to go to the moon."

"Just fly it until the string runs out," Da-Fu said, "then let go."

Minli nodded. It made sense. As they gazed at the wound coil, she said, amused, "It won't take too long for the string to run out, anyway. There is not a lot there!"

"I just hope there is enough for it to fly," A-Fu said.

So, with Da-Fu running, they began to fly the kite. As the kite rose higher and higher, Minli watched the coil of string in her hand.

"Is the string running out yet?" each asked over and over again. But Minli shook her head every time. The thread seemed to endlessly unwind. Even as the kite climbed upward, becoming the size of a name chop mark, the string continued. Slowly, it disappeared from view with the thread scratching the darkening sky with a faint red line.

"That is a magic string," Da-Fu said in an awed voice.

"Of course," the dragon said suddenly. "It's a thread of destiny. If we are destined to see the Old Man of the Moon, it will stretch to reach him."

"You may be destined to meet him, then," A-Fu said, impressed. However, as she looked at the sky turning to night, she frowned. "But we are not. Da-Fu, we should go back home. We have been gone too long. After the Green Tiger, we should try not to worry Amah and A-Gong so much."

"Don't you have anything you want to ask the Old Man of the Moon?" Minli asked. "You could change your fortune too."

"No," Da-A-Fu said, laughing. "Why would we want to change our fortune?"

The children ran down the mountain, their laughter melting into the air. Minli shook her head in confusion, but waved goodbye. As Minli watched them turn into figures of shadows, seeming to dance toward their home and village, she thought of her own Ma and Ba waiting for her in her home far away.

As the sky deepened like brewing tea, Minli and the dragon looked in silence at the red line reaching to the heavens. But just as the moon rose in the darkness, Minli felt a sudden jerk on the string. It began to strain and bend.

"Something's happening!" she cried out.

"Pull the kite in!" Dragon said. "Bring it back!"

"Something has changed!" Minli said as she strained and pulled. "It's heavy now!"

The dragon reached above Minli's head and grabbed the cord. Together, they pulled and dragged. As they strained, Minli wondered if they were bringing down the moon itself.

But there seemed to be no end to the string. As they wound up the thread, it seemed to get thicker and thicker. And when the string became the width of Minli's little finger, a strange clattering — like a wooden wind chime — filled the air.

"Something has happened to the string," the dragon gasped between heaves.

And something strange *had* happened. The thread — which was really now more like a thick silk rope — seemed to have divided itself into a long strange web, reinforced with bamboo stalks. As the endless U-shape came toward them, Minli gasped.

"The string," Minli panted, "it's . . . it's a bridge!"

CHAPTER
40

Ma stood by the window as the stars began to poke holes in the deep, blue velvet sky. The days without Minli had passed slowly, and the evenings even slower. Ma wondered how the silver goldfish could remain calm in the bowl, while she herself felt she could barely breathe. As the night air touched her face, Ma thought of Minli, bit her lip, and sighed. Her eyes closed as she willed her tears to stop forming. When she opened her eyes, Ba was standing next to her.

"I know," he said to her, and he placed his hand over hers.

"It is hard to wait," Ma said.

"Yes," Ba said, "we are like the dragon waiting for a sign of his pearl."

"The dragon waiting?" Ma asked.

"Oh, nothing," Ba said. "It's just a story."

The wind blew gently, like the calming touch of a healer. "I wouldn't mind hearing it," Ma said. "It might make the time pass faster."

Ba looked at her, surprised, and then nodded with a small smile.

THE STORY OF THE DRAGON'S PEARL

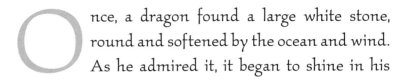

Once, a dragon found a large white stone, round and softened by the ocean and wind. As he admired it, it began to shine in his hands. *How pretty*, he thought. *I will make this into a pearl.*

So day after day, month after month, for many years, the dragon went without eating and sleeping as he made the pearl. He carved the stone with his claws and smoothed it with his scales. He carried it into the clouds, rolled it in fresh raindrops, and bathed it in the Celestial River. He polished it with pale chrysanthemum petals. Finally, it was done — perfectly round and luminously smooth. It was flawless and beautiful. As the dragon looked at it, a tear of exhaustion and joy fell from his eye and landed on the pearl. As the teardrop soaked into the pearl, it began to shine with a dazzling radiance. The dragon smiled with delight. Exhausted, he fell asleep in the light of the pearl.

But the pearl continued to glow. The light was so lovely that it caught the attention of the Queen Mother of the Heavens. When she found out that the brightness came from the dragon's wondrous pearl, she sent two of her servants to steal it. The servants were able to accomplish this quite easily, as the dragon — weary from his many years of work — slept quite long and soundly.

When the Queen Mother received the pearl, even she was astonished by its loveliness. No pearl, no jewel, no treasure in the heavens or on earth could compare. She quickly had a vault made in the deepest part of her kingdom that one could only get to by going through nine locked doors. She put the pearl in the chamber and tied the nine keys to the doors onto her belt.

When the dragon woke up and found his pearl missing, he began a frantic search. He hunted the oceans and mountains, the rivers and valleys. He flew through the Celestial River, examining each star. But none gave the pure, clear light of his pearl.

Eventually, the dragon was forced to give up his search. He had no idea where to look or where the pearl could be. But he did not give up hope that he would find it. Instead, he waited for a sign of it.

And he did not wait in vain. On her birthday, the Queen Mother had a grand celebration. Inviting all the immortals of heaven, she held a "Banquet of Peaches," an endless assortment of rich and delicious dishes made from the peaches of immortality. Fragrant and potent peach wine was served with each dish, and every time her glass was low, the Queen Mother called for more.

So when the guests heralded her with compliments, flattery, and fine gifts, the Queen Mother recklessly decided to show off her stolen treasure. "My dear friends," she said impetuously, "your gifts and words are fine, indeed, but I have something that far outshines them."

And she took out her nine keys, unlocked the nine doors, and brought out the dragon's pearl. A hush went over the party as the pearl glowed with a light of such radiance that it flooded out of the palace and into all the heavens.

As the light broke into the sky, the dragon — ever faithfully alert — jerked up his head. "My pearl!" he said and flew as fast as he could toward the light.

When the dragon reached the Queen Mother's palace, he burst upon a crowd of admiring immortals fawning over the pearl in the hand of the Queen Mother, pompous with pride. "That is my pearl!" he cried. "Give it back!"

The Queen Mother was infuriated. "This is my pearl," she declared, "how dare you!"

"It is mine!" the dragon said, and looking at the flush of her cheeks and evading eyes, demanded, "You stole it, didn't you?"

"I don't need to steal anything," the Queen Mother blustered. "I am the Queen Mother of the Heavens! All treasures made by the earth or heaven belong to me!"

"Heaven did not make that pearl," the dragon said, "nor the earth! I made it with years of work and effort. It is mine!"

The Queen Mother began to panic, and she fled out of the palace and into the garden, clutching the pearl. The dragon pursued her, determined not to lose the pearl again. The party guests followed, creating such a commotion of excitement and chaos that the Heavenly Grandfather (who tended to avoid his daughter's flamboyant parties) decided to leave his study to investigate the disturbance.

The Queen Mother, flustered and agitated, ran through the garden, leading a great chase. As she reached the garden wall and could not run any farther, she was horrified to see not only the dragon and her party guests, but also her father coming after her. As they reached her, in a fit of terror, she threw the pearl over the wall.

The dragon gave a roar of dismay, and all rushed to look over the garden wall to see the pearl fall deep into the Celestial River. In the deep blue water that separated heaven and earth, the pearl seemed to grow larger and glow more radiantly.

The dragon began to make movements to dive into the river when the Heavenly Grandfather stopped him. "Leave it there," he said, "and shame on you both. The pearl should not belong to one being. Do you not see this is where the pearl belongs, where everyone on heaven and earth can see its beauty and enjoy it?"

Both the dragon and the Queen Mother, humbled, nodded and the guests praised the Heavenly Grandfather's wisdom. And so did the people on earth, for now when they looked up into the sky the moon glowed down upon them.

There was a peaceful silence after Ba finished the story. Finally Ma gave a small sigh and a smile. "If Minli were here, she would ask you if that story were true."

"And I would have to tell her, 'probably not,'" Ba said. "When I was a very young boy, I remember seeing a glimpse of a rare dragon pearl. It was being carried to the Emperor himself, guarded by hundreds of men, and there was still a moon in the sky."

"There is more than one pearl in the ocean," the fish said. "So of course there is more than one dragon pearl. Though the dragon pearl that makes the moon is by far the largest."

Ba glanced carefully at the fish and then at Ma, but both seemed ignorant of the other, and neither looked at him.

"I remember hearing about that," Ma said. "That pearl was supposed to be worth the Emperor's entire fortune. A single pearl. I suppose it could've belonged to a dragon."

She spoke without the desire or envy she used to feel when speaking of the wealth of others. The moonlight seemed to transform her, lifting the years of bitterness and hardship and leaving her with a sad serenity. It affected Ba unexpectedly, in a way he had not felt in years; he filled with great tenderness.

But Ma continued to stare dreamily out the window, as unaware of his thoughts as she was of the fish's words.

CHAPTER
41

"It must be a bridge to the top of Never-Ending Mountain," Dragon said, "and to the Old Man of the Moon."

With the attached bamboo stakes, Minli and the dragon had anchored their end of the bridge to the ground. As it stretched into the night, it quivered in the moonlight.

Minli stared at the vast length of the bridge, hanging in the sky like a delicate red spiderweb. "I don't think you will be able to cross it," Minli said.

Dragon, too, looked at the U-shaped bridge, with its

fragile ropes. "I cannot fit on it," he said, "and I doubt it will bear my weight."

"Well," Minli said, "maybe it is magic, like the thread. Try."

Dragon put one foot onto the rope bridge. But as the rope felt his mass, it groaned and the bamboo stakes began to tear out of the ground. Hurriedly, Dragon stepped off.

"I think," Dragon said slowly, "I am not destined to see the Old Man of the Moon."

Minli looked at Dragon's downcast eyes and read the years of sadness and frustration in his face. Tears burned in her eyes as she thought about their long travels that had led to this disappointment.

"I wish I could fly," the dragon said simply.

"You will," Minli said, blinking her tears away. "The bridge is big and strong enough for me. I'll ask the Old Man of the Moon your question and return."

Dragon brightened with hope. "You will?" he asked. "You will do that?"

Minli nodded. "I will wait for you here," Dragon said.

"I will not move until you return. When you tell me what he says, I will fly you back home to your family."

"Then I better get going," Minli said, but her smile faded as she looked at the bridge in front of her that seemed to loom into nothingness.

"I will wait for you here," Dragon repeated.

Minli nodded and took a deep breath. Then, grasping the two side ropes for balance, she carefully stepped onto the rope bridge and began to walk.

CHAPTER
42

The sky around Minli was quiet as she walked on the red rope bridge. The only sounds she heard were those of her own breathing and the pounding of her heart in her chest. After the dragon and land had faded from view, Minli saw nothing except for the night around her. With such a limitless landscape, she could not tell how far she had walked or how much of the bridge she had left. It seemed never ending — she began to wonder if she had walked for hours or days.

But slowly, so slowly Minli almost didn't notice it, the

darkness of the night lessened. With each step she took, the world around her became brighter. And with this light, Minli saw that the sky below her had somehow become a vast lake of pure water and the night clouds were made of floating lilies. And stretched before her in the distance, like a faraway coast, she saw a high wall that seemed to glow. The wall was smooth and creamy white, as if made out of pearl. It too seemed to be endless; Minli could not see where it began or ended.

However, as Minli got closer, she saw a round opening in the wall just before her. And in that circular passageway, a white rabbit stood like a jade statue. It was only when Minli stepped off the bridge and the rabbit started toward her that Minli realized it was alive.

"Welcome," the rabbit said. "You're a little late. Did you have trouble with the monkeys?"

Minli was too astonished to speak. The rabbit looked extremely like the one painted on her blue rice bowl. She nodded with her mouth gaping.

"Well, let's go," the rabbit said. "You're going to have to keep it short with the Old Man; he's very busy and he hates unnecessary talk."

Minli followed the rabbit through the round opening into a white courtyard and over a polished stone bridge that seemed to grow from the ground. As they passed over it, Minli saw the smooth water wave with gentle ripples and heard what sounded like faint drumming. To one side of her in the distance, standing out against the flat landscape, Minli saw the silhouette of a man cutting down a lone tree, his axe making a thumping rhythm. As he chopped, the branches of the tree shook; leaves, blossoms, and seeds flew through the air and dropped into the water like raindrops.

"Is that the Old Man of the Moon?" Minli asked.

"Him?" the rabbit said, following Minli's gaze. "Oh, no. That's Wu Kang."

"Why is he cutting down the tree?" Minli asked. It seemed a shame to her that the only tree on Never-Ending Mountain was being cut down.

"Questions, questions," the rabbit said. "I should make you wait to ask the Old Man, but if you must know, Wu Kang tries to cut down that tree every night."

"Every night?" Minli couldn't help asking.

"Yes," the rabbit said.

THE STORY OF WU KANG

Most thought Wu Kang was very lucky. His wife was beautiful and his children were healthy and they all lived in a comfortable cottage on a farm in the country. His parents and elder brother lived with him, and his neighbors were faithful friends. But Wu Kang always wanted more. So when his crops thrived and flourished, he decided farming was not satisfying enough for him and the day he reaped his successful harvest, he told his friends that he was leaving the countryside to move to town.

"Why?" they asked him.

"I want more," Wu Kang said.

"But we are so happy here all together," they said.

"It is not enough," Wu Kang said.

So he packed up his possessions, and sold his cottage, farm, and land. Then, with his wife, children, parents, and brother, he moved to town. It was crowded and inconvenient in the smaller house, but Wu Kang was able to apprentice himself to a furniture maker, and his family began to adapt to their cramped home. However, the day he was able to carve a chair from beechwood was the day he quit and decided to move to the city.

"Why?" his parents asked him.

"I want more," Wu Kang said.

"But we are happy here together," they said.

"It is not enough," Wu Kang said.

So, with his wife and children walking behind him, Wu Kang left his parents and brother behind and moved to the city to search for something more. Their new home was a small hut of earth squeezed between other tumbledown houses on a filthy street, far away from the tight, cozy house in town or the comfortable cottage on the farm. Nonetheless, his wife and children adjusted to life in the city while Wu Kang looked for satisfaction. But still nothing was enough for him. After mastering the abacus, Wu Kang decided to quit the training to be a storekeeper. After learning how to

hold a paintbrush, he stopped studying for a government position. Wu Kang always wanted more.

"Maybe you should try to become an Immortal,"
his young son said to him. "You couldn't want more
than that."

"I think," Wu Kang said, "perhaps, you are right."

So Wu Kang packed up a small bag and left his wife
and children to find an Immortal to study under. His
heartbroken wife pleaded with him as he stepped out
the door.

"Don't leave," she said. "Here, we are together."

"It is not enough," Wu Kang said.

Wu Kang searched and traveled long and far and,
one night, he found the Old Man of the Moon. "At
last," Wu Kang said, "an Immortal! Master, will you
teach me?"

The Old Man of the Moon preferred to decline, but
Wu Kang insisted and begged. So, with misgivings,
the Old Man agreed and brought Wu Kang to Never-
Ending Mountain.

So the Old Man began to teach Wu Kang lessons

full of wonder, that common men would marvel at. However, Wu Kang, true to his nature, was unmoved and aspired for more. When the Old Man showed him how to obtain red threads from his granddaughter, the Goddess of Weaving, traveling across the sea of stars on a bridge of night birds, Wu Kang watched and followed but, after three days, was discontent. "Master," Wu Kang said, "there must be something more you can teach me."

So the Old Man taught Wu Kang how to tie the threads of destiny, sealing the knots with a shaft of light from the moon. Wu Kang studied and copied, but after two days he again grew restless. "Master," Wu Kang said, "I know you can teach me more."

Hence, the Old Man took out the sacred Book of Fortune and began to teach Wu Kang how to read its text. But after one day, Wu Kang exclaimed, "There must be more than this!"

With that, the Old Man clapped the book shut. "Yes," the Old Man agreed, "there is."

And without a word, the Old Man led Wu Kang to a barren area of Never-Ending Mountain. The Old Man knocked the ground with his walking stick and from the rock a silver tree grew. As Wu Kang stared, the Old Man tied a string of destiny around him and the tree.

"The only things for me to teach you," the Old Man said to Wu Kang as he handed him an axe, "are the lessons of contentment and patience. Only when you are able to cut this tree down will I know you have learned them."

Wu Kang shrugged and began in earnest to chop down the tree. Little did he realize that with every cut the tree grew back, and every blow only scattered the seeds from the tree into the night sky lake.

So every night Wu Kang cuts the tree. Tied by the string of destiny, he cannot leave it and is fated to chop until he learns his lesson or until the end of time.

Minli walked silently after the rabbit finished the story, and for a while the only sounds were of the tree's flying seeds falling into the water.

Those seeds, Minli said to herself, *they are really falling through the sky to the earth. They are the seeds that fall onto Moon Rain Village! It's Wu Kang's chopping that makes the strange moon rain. The flowering trees grow from the seeds from the tree on Never-Ending Mountain . . .*

But just then Minli's thoughts were interrupted by the rabbit, which had stopped suddenly.

"In there," the rabbit said, motioning toward a circular opening through a stone wall, "is the Old Man of the Moon."

CHAPTER

43

Minli took one step into the walled courtyard and then stopped. Countless red threads covered the ground like intricate lace. Interwoven in the red strings were thousands and thousands of small clay figures, each no longer than her finger; like a spider, in the exact center, sat the Old Man of the Moon.

He sat cross-legged, with a giant book on his lap. His head was bowed over two clay figures in his hand, so that the most that Minli saw of him was the top of his head. But she could see his delicate, wrinkled hands, skillfully tying the figures in his lap together with a red thread. A blue silk bag full of red strings lay open beside him, and Minli felt a shock run through her as she saw it. She had seen that bag before! Deep blue silk, silver embroidery — it was the bag the buffalo boy's friend had been carrying that starry night. *She's the Goddess of Weaving!* Minli realized. *She spins the red thread for the Old Man of the Moon. I knew there was something different about her. No wonder she knew how to find the king.*

The Old Man reached beside him for his walking stick — a bent, twisted wood stick — and tapped it on the ground. Silently, the clay figures floated from his hand, drifted in the air, then settled to the ground at opposite ends of the courtyard. The Old Man's thread still connected them and the red line wove itself among the other strands surrounding him.

As Minli stared, the Old Man looked at her. The silver hair of his beard seemed to flow like a glowing waterfall and disappear into the folds of his robes, and his dark eyes matched the blackness of the night sky.

"Ah," the Old Man said, "it's you."

Minli nodded and bowed deeply. She would have

kneeled on the ground, but she was afraid of disrupting the clay figures standing on the ground at her feet.

"Well, come here, then," the Old Man said impatiently, and he tapped his stick on the ground again. And with a sound like a flapping of a bird's wing, the clay figures moved — clearing a path for Minli.

"I know you have questions for me," the Old Man said. "Every ninety-nine years, someone comes here with their questions. But I will answer only one. So choose your question carefully."

One question! Minli almost stopped walking in shock. If she was only allowed to ask one question, she could not ask Dragon's question for him! Unless . . . she did not ask her own.

Minli felt like a fish gasping for air. What was she going to do? The memories of the hard work in the rice fields, her father's careworn hands, the plain rice in the dinner bowls, and Ma's sighs washed upon her like the splashes of water from the lake. She had to change her fortune; she must ask how to do that.

But when Minli thought about Dragon, waiting for her patiently, it was as if she had been struck. And like seeds falling from Wu Kang's tree, images of the Dragon rained upon her — their laughter as they passed the monkeys, his awkward struggles walking in the woods, his echoing roar as he flung the Green Tiger into the air, the kind hand he put on her shoulder when she cried, and the hopeful look in his eyes as she left. *Dragon is my friend,* Minli said to herself. *What should I do?*

Minli's thoughts bubbled faster and faster like boiling rice; every step she took seemed to throb and Minli wasn't sure if the pounding was her heart or Wu Kang's axe in the distance. As she passed the clay statues, she thought she could see figures of the goldfish man, the buffalo boy, the king, and Da-A-Fu silently watching her. Minli's feet seemed to ignore her pleas for slowness; like the kite being pulled in, she was being drawn toward the Old Man of the Moon without delay. Before she could decide whose question to ask, Minli found herself facing him.

The Old Man of the Moon looked at her expectantly, his black eyes as unreadable as the night sky. Minli looked down into the open book on his lap. She recognized the open page as the king's borrowed line — the smoothed-out folds and the holes she had made in it when she had turned it into a kite were still there. Yet, now the paper was invisibly fastened in the book, with only a thin line, like a scar, showing that it had ever been removed.

And the words had changed again. There was a single line of words running down the entire page. As she looked, Minli realized for the first time, she could read the words — or really the word. For the line was only made of one word, written over and over again. And that word was *Thankfulness.*

And suddenly, like the light when the clouds move away from the moon, Minli knew clearly what question to ask.

"There is a dragon waiting at the bridge," she said. "Why can he not fly?"

CHAPTER
44

Ma and Ba continued to wait for Minli, quietly and sadly. Even though they told themselves that they trusted Minli and believed she would return, Ma spent most of her time looking out the window, lost in thought, while Ba grew older and grayer every day. The only time they found comfort was in the evenings, when Ba would tell a story to make the time pass faster. In the escape of Ba's tales, they could forget that Minli was not with them and imagine that she was there listening.

One evening, when the moon filled the sky, Ma spoke.

"Husband," she said, "tonight, I would like to tell you a story."

Ba was slightly surprised, but nodded.

THE STORY THAT MA TOLD

Once there was a woman who had a kind husband and a beautiful daughter. A great mountain shadowed their home, making the land that they lived on poor and their house small. But there was always enough to eat, and the water always flowed in hot months, while a fire always burned during the cold ones. Yet the woman was not content.

The woman begrudged the barren mountain and the meager land and swallowed her plain rice with bitterness. She frowned at the humble cotton of their clothes and sighed in resentment at the tight rooms of the house.

Day after day, the woman grumbled. When she heard stories of treasures of gold and jade, she was filled with envy. "Why do we have nothing?" She sulked in frustration. "We have no treasures, no fortune. Why are we so poor?"

Her husband and daughter worked harder every day, hoping to bring wealth to their house. But the unfeeling land did not cooperate, and the house remained cramped, the clothes stayed modest, and there was always only just enough rice for the three of them. The woman also remained unhappy; her displeasure grew like weeds — uncontrollable and tangling.

The woman was so caught up in her dissatisfaction, she did not realize that she was planting seeds of discontent in her daughter as well. Until then, her daughter had been pleased with their life, but now she began to feel troubled. The rice that filled their bowls began to taste bland, the clothes she had liked for their colors now felt rough, and the house that she had run freely around in had become stifling.

Finally, unable to bear the growing frustration, the daughter stole away in the middle of the night —

vowing not to return until she could bring a fortune back to her family.

And it was only then that the woman saw the stupidity of her behavior. For without her daughter, the house became too large and empty, and she was not hungry for the extra rice. As the days passed in loneliness, fear, and worry, the woman cursed herself for her selfishness and foolishness. How lucky she had been! She was at last able to see that her daughter's laughter and love could not be improved by having the finest clothes or jewels, that joy had been in her home like a gift waiting to be opened. The woman wept tears for which there was no comfort. For all the time that she had been longing for treasures, she had already had the one most precious.

Now wiser, the woman could do nothing but go to her husband, beg forgiveness for her actions, and hope to someday do the same with her daughter. She did not know if she would receive compassion from either, but she vowed she would wait for it. If necessary she would wait like the mountain that shadowed them.

As Ma finished, she sat herself down at Ba's feet and, like a child, she placed her head in his lap.

"Husband," she said, "I've said it was your fault that Minli ran away and I was wrong. I am to blame. Minli knew I was discontent with our fortune; if I had not been, she would not have left. I am sorry."

Ba could not speak. The moon outside was so full it looked as if it would burst, and moistness dampened his eyes. He placed his hand tenderly on Ma's head.

"Ahh, good," the fish said. "If you make happy those that are near, those that are far will come."

Ma's head raised in a jerk. She looked over at the fish and then looked at Ba, her eyes wide.

"Did the fish say something?" she asked.

CHAPTER
45

The dragon waited. Mornings rose, nights fell, but he did not move from the bridge. Every night the stars filled the sky like snowflakes falling on black stone and then melted away as the sun mounted. When the sun rose, the red strings of the bridge melted into the sky and the bridge seemed to disappear, only showing itself again at night. A stinging wind blew in a silver mist and the cold rock was hard and unyielding. Still the dragon waited.

But on the third night, just as the moon began to slip down in the sky, Dragon saw a faint figure on the bridge.

With a joyous roar, the dragon jumped up and the figure became clearer and clearer. Minli!

"You are back!" Dragon shouted. "Did you see him? Did you ask the Old Man of the Moon my question?"

"Yes, yes," Minli laughed as she hugged the dragon, "I asked him. And he answered. So now I know! I know how you can fly!"

"How?" Dragon asked.

Minli climbed onto Dragon's back. With both hands, she clenched the stone ball above his head.

"Take a deep breath," she said to him; and with a jerk that took all her strength, she yanked the ball off his head.

"Ouch!" Dragon yelped. But then, he began to smile. "I feel so light," he said, "so light and peaceful."

"The Old Man of the Moon said you would not be able to fly until the ball was removed from your head," Minli told him. "He said it was weighing you down."

"It was!" Dragon laughed and Minli clutched his neck with her spare arm as he rose into the air. The wind seemed to join their whoop of laughter and sweep them up into the sky as the dragon flew for the first time. The silver clouds embraced them and then parted as the dragon flew through, as if he were rippling the sky; the pale moon looked as if it were smiling at them with a soft glow. As they skimmed the stars, Minli closed her eyes with delight.

As they returned to the ground, the dragon asked, "What about you? Did the Old Man tell you how to change your fortune?"

Minli was silent. Dragon turned to look at her.

"What happened?" he asked. "He did not tell you?"

"I didn't ask," Minli said. "I was only allowed one question."

"What?" the dragon said. "You need to know! You have come all this way. We will fly back and you can ask him!"

Before Minli could utter a protest, the red cord bridge seemed to shriek, and as they turned to look at it, the bamboo stakes began to rip the ground, leaving ugly slashes as the bridge was dragged away from the land. The bridge jerked violently, the bamboo supports clattering as it was pulled up into the darkness.

"The Old Man of the Moon will not see me again," Minli said. "He won't answer any question for another ninety-nine years."

"But, you . . . ," the dragon sputtered, "your fortune, your parents . . ."

"It's all right," Minli told him. "When it was time for me to choose, I suddenly saw I didn't have to ask it."

"You did not?" the dragon said.

"No," Minli said, and suddenly memories rushed through her. She heard the buffalo boy's laughter as he refused her money, saw the king's generous smile as he willingly parted with his family's treasure, and remembered Da-A-Fu's last words to her. "Why would we want to change our fortune?" they had said. She had shaken her head in confusion then, but now, finally, Minli understood all of it. Fortune was not a house full of gold and jade, but something much more. Something she already had and did not need to change. "I didn't ask the question," Minli said again and smiled, "because I don't need to know the answer."

CHAPTER
46

The moon began to fade as the brightening sky revealed itself through it. The sun was awakening, and Minli wanted to return home as soon as possible. Dragon, having waited three days and nights, was well rested, so they decided to leave Never-Ending Mountain at once.

As Dragon soared through the sky, any heaviness inside Minli left. He seemed to dance in the air, and his happiness made her feel as light as the clouds around her. The sun seemed to warm her heart and joy bubbled inside of her. She knew she had asked the right question.

Before they left, Minli and the dragon circled over the Village of the Moon Rain. Da-A-Fu, Amah, A-Gong, and the villagers saw them and ran out of their stone hut, flapping their ruined sleeves in greeting. "Don't stop," Amah shouted with a broad smile, "go home!" Minli nodded and waved goodbye until the flowering trees looked like brush strokes of golden paint on the mountain.

Flying on the dragon made traveling much faster. It seemed as if in no time they were above the City of Bright Moonlight — from the sky, the Inner City and Outer City grids looked like a giant labyrinth, and the two stone guardians looked as if they were dog trinkets molded from clay. Minli saw the roof of the buffalo boy's broken-down hut, but no glimpse of him. *He's probably inside, sleeping,* Minli thought, wondering if the Goddess of Weaving had visited the previous night.

But as they passed the bay of water by the city, Minli saw something strange, like an orange shadow streaking across the sky. Dragon saw it too and slowed down. As it got closer, there was no mistaking it. It was another dragon!

The dragon was orange, the color of the inside of a ripe

mango. When she saw Minli and Dragon, a coquettish smile spread across her face.

"Hello," Dragon breathed in an odd voice. Minli looked at him in surprise.

But the orange dragon kept flying without saying a word. As she passed, she winked at them. Dragon balanced in mid-air as if stunned. He watched the orange dragon sweep down and away to the water below until she was a ginger speck in the distance.

"Are you okay?" Minli asked the dragon as he continued to stare. "You must be excited that you've finally seen another dragon."

"I am," Dragon said, as if in a daze. Then he shook himself as if trying to rouse himself awake. "But I will find her again later. I will bring you home first."

Minli shrugged. Dragon was acting oddly. But there was something familiar about that orange dragon, perhaps the way her scales reflected in the sun like fish scales glistening in the water, and those knowledgeable eyes, nodding as if she knew her. Minli smiled.

Hours passed and the land below them blurred. Minli slept on and off; the smooth ride of the flying dragon made it easy for her to sleep. Minli was impressed by how far they had journeyed and how much faster they were able to travel by flying. The sun was only beginning to go down past the horizon when they saw the edge of the peach forest. The tops of the peach trees seemed to sway a welcome to them as they flew overhead, and as they continued to fly, Minli thought she saw the monkeys still attached by the fishnet around the pot of rice.

But Dragon was still acting strangely. When Fruitless Mountain, with its familiar black peak cutting into the pink and orange sunset sky, came into view, the dragon almost stopped flying.

"What mountain is that?" he asked Minli.

"It's Fruitless Mountain," Minli told him. "Right beyond it, next to the Jade River, is my home."

"Fruitless Mountain," he said to himself, and even though he continued to fly, he seemed to be in a daze. Minli wondered if flying had somehow made him lightheaded. But her attention could not be kept by her concern for him. Night was falling and the dark lines of Fruitless Mountain softened in the shadowy sky. But Minli could still see that every moment brought the Jade River and Fruitless Mountain closer. She was almost home!

However, when they reached Fruitless Mountain, Dragon suddenly stopped. He dropped lightly to the base of Fruitless Mountain, where so long ago Minli had taken some stone to make her compass.

"This is Fruitless Mountain," Dragon said, and again Minli looked at him. He was definitely acting out of the ordinary.

"Yes," Minli said, a bit puzzled. "My village is just a bit past this. I can walk from here if you wish."

"Do you mind?" Dragon asked. "For some reason, I feel as if I do not want to leave here."

"No, I don't mind," Minli said. "Are you okay?"

The dragon looked at her and smiled. "Yes," Dragon said. "Strangely, I feel like I am home."

Minli wrinkled her forehead in confusion, but was too eager to get home to her parents to ask any more questions. Minli hugged Dragon goodbye. He returned her hug warmly, but she could tell he was distracted. She held out the round ball she had taken from Dragon's head. "Do you want this?"

"No." Dragon glanced at it absentmindedly. "You can have it."

Minli shrugged again, but the urge to go home began to pull at her strongly. She waved goodbye to Dragon and began to run toward the village.

It was late at night when she finally reached home. The slumbering village was silent, and as Minli crept into her home the pale goldfish greeted her.

"Shh," the goldfish said to her. "Your parents are sleeping. Welcome home."

Minli was a little surprised to see a goldfish, but smiled a greeting. Moonlight misted over the rough floors and made the sparse room glow silver, the goldfish bowl looking like a second moon. The shabby walls and worn stones seemed to shimmer as if a translucent silk veil covered them, muting any flaws and transforming the house into a dwelling of luminous light and delicate shadows. Minli had never seen her home look so beautiful.

Tiptoeing, she put her bag and the dragon's stone on the table and went into her room. Smiling, she climbed into her bed and went to sleep.

CHAPTER

47

"Minli? Minli!" Ma and Ba's happiness burst from them like exploding firecrackers and even before she could open her eyes they had flung themselves upon her. The joy! How it flowed and flooded over her! More golden than the king's dragon bracelet, sweeter than a peach from the Queen Mother's garden, and more beautiful than a Goddess of Heaven! Minli smiled, treasuring her good fortune.

Ma and Ba only stopped hugging her when her stomach began to grumble with hunger. Ma rushed to make a special breakfast, taking out the carefully saved dried pork to make Minli's favorite porridge, while Ba jumped to get some fresh water to make tea.

But when Ba went into the main room, he made a choking noise that caused Minli and Ma to come running.

"What is that?" he said, pointing. Minli followed his finger and saw him pointing at her traveling possessions on the table. The fish swam merrily around in its bowl as the silk of her brocade bag made the sunlight skip around the room.

"That is a bag given to me by the King of the City of Bright Moonlight," Minli said. "It is very fine, isn't it?"

"Not that," Ba said, waving the bag away. "That!"

And now Minli saw that he was pointing to Dragon's stone ball.

"It's just a gift from a friend," Minli said, handing it to her father. Ba took it in his hands reverently, a look of awe on his face.

"This is not just any gift," Ba whispered, and he took his sleeve and gently rubbed the surface of the stone. To

Minli's great surprise, the grayness of the stone began to smudge away and a translucent, lustrous glow seemed to shine through. "This is a dragon's pearl."

Minli and Ma stared. "A dragon's pearl!" Ma said slowly. She sat down and looked at Minli. "A dragon's pearl is worth the Emperor's entire fortune."

Minli opened her mouth but before any words could come out there was a great shouting and clamoring outside on the street. Ba quickly, but carefully, put the dragon pearl back on the table before they all hurried out to see what the uproar was about.

"What is it?" Ma asked, grabbing a neighbor. The entire village had flowed into the street, talking and shouting like a flock of birds discovering a feast. "What is happening?"

"It's Fruitless Mountain!" the neighbor said. "Fruitless Mountain has turned green."

"What?" Ba said.

"It's true, it's true!" another neighbor chimed in. "Fruitless Mountain is no longer fruitless! And the Jade River is clear and fresh too!"

Minli, Ma, and Ba looked at the mountain. It was true.

Fruitless Mountain was no longer a black shadow above them. As the day dawned, the mountain had transformed. A green lushness seemed to bloom from the rock — a jewel-colored splendor softened the sharp edges that had painfully sliced the sky. The sky itself seemed to be embracing the mountain. The wind softly caressed the newborn greenery with a nurturing breeze and skimmed the Jade River, the water now as clear as tears of joy.

"How is this possible?" Ma asked.

"Jade Dragon must be happy again," Ba said. "Perhaps she is reunited with one of her dragon children."

Dragon! Minli thought, and her quick-thinking mind seemed to spin. Dragon said he was making his home on Fruitless Mountain. Could he be one of Jade Dragon's children? But how? Dragon was born from a painting, from paintbrushes and inkstones . . . and like an echo, Minli remembered Ma talking about the artist who had come to Fruitless Mountain many years ago. *He took the mountain rock to carve into inking stones.*

Perhaps Dragon was born from an inkstone made of Fruitless Mountain, the heart of Jade Dragon. Then perhaps he *was* one of Jade Dragon's children. And by bringing him to Fruitless Mountain, Minli had discovered how to make Fruitless Mountain green again.

"Minli!" A villager, finally recovered from the shock of the green mountain, stared at Minli. "You came back! Look, everyone! Minli has returned!"

As the neighbors clamored around, Ma sighed. But it was a sigh of joy, a sound of happiness that floated like a butterfly in the air. "Good fortune has come to the village," Ma said, smiling. "And to us, as well."

"Yes," Ba said, looking affectionately at Minli. "But the best fortune is the one that returned."

Minli smiled back. And suddenly, as she thought about her journey to and from Never-Ending Mountain, Minli realized that while she had not asked the Old Man of the Moon any of her questions, they all had been answered.

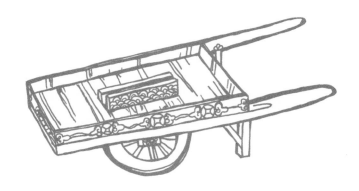

CHAPTER
48

The goldfish man shaded his eyes as he pushed his cart along the Jade River. Yes, he was almost there. How long had it been? Two years? Perhaps three. *Yes, the poor Village of Fruitless Mountain should be ahead soon,* he thought.

But, possibly, he was mistaken. When he had been there last, the most striking characteristic of the landscape had been the black mountain, its shadow casting gloom upon the village. But there was no dark silhouette in the sky now; in fact, the landscape looked as if it were from a heavenly painting. A majestic green mountain sat in harmony with the deepening blue sky, the sun spreading its light for the last time before it set. Had he taken a wrong turn somewhere?

As he gazed, two flying figures in the sky caught his eye. Red and orange, a dragon and his mate frolicking amongst the clouds . . . wait, dragons? The goldfish man shook his head in disbelief, rubbed his eyes, and looked again. Only the dimming sky and feathery clouds fanning the wind were above. *I must have been imagining things,* he thought.

The goldfish man pushed onward. The water in the fishbowls rippled and waved as the fish gazed calmly; their brilliant colors against the abundant green land glinted like gold and jade.

As he entered the village, the goldfish man again began to doubt if he was in the right place. Smooth stone lined the roadway and, instead of the rough board houses he remembered, rich wooden doors — some elaborately carved — lined the street. As he pushed his cart down the narrow street, lively children dressed in gay colors flew toward him like a festival of silk kites. "Goldfish! Goldfish!" they cried. "Ma! Ba! Can we get one?"

Parents walked over and smiled indulgently at their children, and by the time the sun disappeared, the goldfish man had sold out of his wares. Clearly this was not the same poor village he had come to before, where only that one girl purchased a fish.

But then he remembered hearing a story about how a family that lived by the Jade River had given the King of the City of Bright Moonlight the incredible gift of a Dragon Pearl, refusing any payment. In gratitude, the king presented the entire village with gifts of seeds and farming equipment that brought more prosperity than any reward of gold and jade. Maybe this was the place.

"Little one," the goldfish man asked a young girl dressed in a peony-pink silk jacket and leaf-green pantaloons, "the last time I was here, the last time I came to the Village of Fruitless Mountain, a child ran away from home. What happened to her?"

"Ran away from here?" the girl looked at him in disbelief, as if the idea was foreign. Then she nodded. "Oh, you must mean Minli! That's when this used to be called the

Village of Fruitless Mountain. Now it's called the Village of Fruitful Mountain."

"Yes, Minli," the goldfish man said. "I think that was her name. What happened to her?"

"She and her family live over there." The girl waved her arm. "They built a courtyard in front and in back of their house. It's behind the gate with the pictures of the lucky children on the door."

The goldfish man wheeled his empty cart to the indicated gate. On each half of the crimson doors hung a painting of a round-faced, laughing child dressed in brilliant red. Their pink cheeks and merry smiles made it impossible not to smile back, and as he grasped one of the metal door knockers shaped like a grinning lion head, he realized that the painting on the left was of a girl and the one on the right was a boy.

The door flew open as soon as he knocked and the goldfish man was face-to-face with a woman he scarcely recognized. He recognized her even less when she threw her arm around him like an old friend.

"You!" she said to him, her face wrinkling in cheerful

smiles. "Come in, come in! My husband will be happy to see you."

The goldfish man, speechless with surprise, let himself be led through the gate doors. Was this the mother with angry eyes he had met in the woods long ago? Yes, this pleasant-faced woman, her plum-colored coat embroidered with flowering trees, was the same person. He shook his head in disbelief.

As he glanced upward, he realized the courtyard was like a well for the sky — the stars and night seemed to flow into it endlessly. *Was the courtyard built for just that purpose?* he wondered. Light from the house streamed through the lattice-patterned doors, illuminating the enclosure like a lit lantern. There, the father was surrounded by visiting children, whom the goldfish man recognized as his earlier customers. Some of the children were playing on the ground with clay toys of boys, buffalo, monkeys, and rabbits while others were being served tea by the father. "This tea is a gift from our faraway friends," the father was saying as he handed a child a cup. "They call it Dragon Well . . ."

"Husband," the woman called. "Husband! Look who is here!"

As he caught sight of the goldfish man, the father stopped in mid-sentence, and his face broke into a wide smile. "Ah!" he cried. "Dear friend!"

And like the mother, before letting him bow politely, the father embraced him warmly. "Come," the father said, "have some tea. My wife will bring out some cakes and snacks."

The goldfish man finally found his voice. "I am glad to see you and your wife so happy and prosperous," he said. "I only stopped to see if . . . last time we met . . . how is your daughter?"

"Minli?" the father said, laughing, waving his hand toward the house. "She is in the back. She will be happy to see you too, but she will come out later. This is the time of night she likes to watch the moon."

"She returned, then?" the goldfish man asked. "I thought she would. What happened?"

"Ah, my friend." Ba laughed again. "You have come at the right time. Why do you think these children are here?

They come here every night because they want to hear the story again — the story of Minli's journey to and from Never-Ending Mountain! Come, sit! You can hear it for the first time."

The goldfish man sat down willingly on a stone seat and found a fragrant cup of tea in his hand. The children clamored around Ba, each more excited than the last and eager for the story to begin. But as Ma went inside the house to get refreshments, she left the door wide open and the goldfish man could not help peering in.

He could see all the way through the house to the back courtyard, where the figure of a young girl sat on a bench, a small pond of fish at her feet. The moonlight washed over everything like a rich bath of gold and silver, making the fish shimmer like pearls and the girl glow with a magical glory reserved for the stars of heaven. But Minli was obviously unaware of all around her, lost in faraway dreams. For even in the misty light, the goldfish man could see her smiling a secret smile up to the sky to where the mountain meets the moon.

READER'S GUIDE

1. Stories are an important part of Minli's life. What does Ma think about stories? Why do you think she feels that way? Are your parents more like Ma or like Ba?

2. When Minli sets off on her journey, she writes a letter to Ma and Ba, and she signs it "Love, your obedient daughter." Is Minli being obedient or disobedient at that moment? In what ways are her actions similar to or different from the actions of Jade Dragon's children? Have you ever been faced with decisions like the ones Minli and Jade Dragon's children have to make?

3. After Dragon finishes his story, he seems sad that he is not a "real" dragon. Minli tries to cheer him up by saying that he feels real to her and they can at least be real friends. What does it mean to have a real friend? What qualities do you look for in a real friend?

4. In the story told by the goldfish man, Ma and Ba learn that he once read from the Book of Fortune. If you had the chance

to read from the Book of Fortune, would you do it? Why or why not?

5. As Ma and Ba think about whether they should let Minli try to change their fortune, Ba says it is like trying to find the paper of happiness. In the story he tells, the secret of happiness is shared but then lost. What do you think was written on the missing paper? What one word might be the secret to happiness? Why do you think this?

6. When Minli meets the buffalo boy and is taken to his home, she feels a tightness in her throat when she thinks of her home in contrast with the boy's home. What does she have that the buffalo boy does not have? What does the buffalo boy have that she does not have?

7. Minli is faced with a difficult decision when she reaches the Old Man of the Moon. She can ask only one question. Which question does she ask? Why does she ask that question? What question would you ask the Old Man of the Moon?

8. Ma says stories are worthless, but stories play an important role throughout Minli's adventure. How did stories help

Minli and others reach their goals? How did stories help characters change and develop throughout the book? Do you think stories are important?

9. Many stories are told within the main story of *Where the Mountain Meets the Moon*. Which was your favorite?

10. If you could meet one of the characters in this book, who would it be? Why? What would you talk about?

BEHIND THE STORY

I grew up as the only Asian in my elementary school classroom and one of the few minorities in my town (very much how it is written in my book *The Year of the Dog*). By the age of eleven, I had fully disregarded my Asian heritage. My wise mother, knowing that any type of forced cultural exposure would lead to scorn, silently left half a dozen Chinese folktale and fairy-tale books on the shelf. Unable to resist the pull of new books, I very quietly began to read them.

At first I was disappointed. The translation from Chinese to English had left the stories extremely thin and at times rough and hard to understand. There were hardly any details or de-scriptions, and the black-and-white illustrations were simple line drawings, a far cry from the lush paintings in my books of European fairy tales. I thought these Chinese stories had not made an impression on me.

But I was wrong. As I grew older, I began to regret my childhood disinterest in my heritage. I visited Hong Kong, Taiwan, and China, and suddenly, those stories came flood-ing back to me. In the land and architecture around me, the Chinese fairy tales seemed to come alive. Everything I saw brought back memories of those stories.

I began to add my own details to the stories. My imagination ignored dynasties and historical elements, and I filled the stories with my own fanciful layers until they became something original—a new story inspired by the myths I had read and the images I saw in my travels. For example, in China I visited the mountain village of Chuadixia:

I used the image in my sketch:

And that eventually became the cold mountain village of Moon Rain:

There were many other inspirations. The Humble Administrator's Garden I saw in Suzhou became the City of Bright Moonlight's Palace Garden:

And the rock sculptures I saw at YuYuan Garden became the inspiration for Minli's hiding place:

Of course, other inspirations were the myths themselves. I embellished some myths only slightly. For example, the Old Man of the Moon is very much Yue-lao—the Chinese God of Marriage (sometimes called the Old Man Under the Moon) with a little bit of Shou Xing, the God of Longevity, mixed in. Yue-lao carries a book of knowledge and a bag of red thread, which he uses to tie future spouses together—just like the Old Man of the Moon does. I, however, expanded the role of those threads so that they not only tied together those destined to marry, but also all those destined to meet.

Other characters were given much more invention. In my youth, I was always curious about the two lucky children displayed on doorways during the Lunar New Year. Who were these children, and why were they lucky? I searched for answers but was able to find only a small tidbit. These decorations were in the image of a pair of children called Da-A-Fu. According to legend, they were sent from the heavens to vanquish a green beast that was terrorizing a village. There were no details on what kind of beast it was or how the children succeeded. So I created the characters of A-Fu and Da-Fu and had them destroy the evil Green Tiger of my own imagination.

This is also why, at the end of the book, I have images of A-Fu and Da-Fu displayed on Minli's doors—a hint of the inspiration for their characters.

Some things were completely my own inventions. For example, the lions that come to life, the red cord bridge, and Fruitless Mountain turning green were not based on any specific folktales—though many similar elements can probably be found. In fact, many times I found myself unsure which elements were my own fabrications and which were the traditional stories!

That is, of course, how I hope the book is for you. All these stories and images are the threads that tie together to make *Where the Mountain Meets the Moon*. It is a fantasy inspired by the Chinese folktales that enchanted me in my youth and the land and culture that fascinates me in my adulthood. I hope there is magic in it for you as well.

GRACE LIN is the award-winning author and illustrator of many novels, including *Starry River of the Sky* and *The Year of the Dog*, as well as picture books such as *The Ugly Vegetables* and *Dim Sum for Everyone! Where the Mountain Meets the Moon* was partially inspired by Grace's travels to Hong Kong, China, and Taiwan, where this photo (also an inspired fantasy!) was taken. Grace lives in Massachusetts. Her website is gracelin.com.

★ **"REMARKABLE."**
—*Booklist* (starred review)

"GENTLE, APPEALING . . . ENGAGING." —*Kirkus Reviews*

A *Publishers Weekly* Best Book of the Year
★ **"MESMERIZING."** —*Booklist* (starred review)
★ **"EXQUISITE".** —*Kirkus Reviews* (starred review)
★ **"ENCHANTING."** —*School Library Journal* (starred review)